By All Mean$

By All Mean$

Bobby "BJ" Austin

authorHOUSE®

AuthorHouse™
1663 Liberty Drive
Bloomington, IN 47403
www.authorhouse.com
Phone: 1-800-839-8640

First published by AuthorHouse   01/17/2012

ISBN: 978-1-4685-4294-3 (sc)
ISBN: 978-1-4685-4293-6 (ebk)

Library of Congress Control Number: 2012900729

Printed in the United States of America

Any people depicted in stock imagery provided by Thinkstock are models,
and such images are being used for illustrative purposes only.
Certain stock imagery © Thinkstock.

This book is printed on acid-free paper.

Front Cover Design: BJ Austin
Back Cover Photo: Christi Ikeda (As I see You Photography)
Proofread and Editing: Jessica Wilkerson

Dedication and Acknowledgment

I would like to thank you for taking the time to read my book. I was inspired to write while serving time in prison. At first, angry because I felt I was given an unfair punishment. As the years progressed I thought about how I ended up in prison. I was just trying to be the best I can be which was hard with strikes against me, who wants to hire an ex-felon. As a man, not being able to "do" did not sit well with me. I was the man of my mother's house so that was not cool for me at all and wasn't a good look. So I decided I needed to do whatever it took to get the ball rolling. Even though I was not doing exactly what the characters did, I was still in some way being a menace to society. I made some bad decisions in my life and realize there are other young men struggling with this thing called man hood and turn to the streets, their daddy. The streets persuaded me into believing that they would always have my back and I will always have the finer things in life. Yeah right. The minute I got locked up the streets were nowhere to be found. No bond money, no phone calls, no visits, no letters; the streets left me hanging with a 25 year sentence. But guess who I did have? My mother and my sister were there then and they are still here. This book is dedicated to my mother, Marinda

Austin and my sister, Jessica Wilkerson. Thank you from the bottom of my heart. I'm better because of you two and the change of heart by God. I also want to dedicate this to some young lost boy who is trying to figure it out on your own. Maybe your father was never there to guide you and chastise you when you needed to be. In my case, mine passed away when I was 8 years old. I was angry for years. But change took place and you don't have to be another statistic. Just know that you can make it without the streets.

Contents

In the Beginning

"Lay y'all bitch ass face down on the ground," the armed gunman yelled at the three dudes standing in front of him. "Man what's going on?" one of the dudes asked nervously while making his way to the ground. "Nigga, you must be stupid" the gunman said. "Stand yo bitch ass back up!" he ordered. The dude stood up with his hands in the air. "Say just watch these fools while we go to the back" the gunman said to his assistant. "Alright bet" he replied. The head gunman grabbed the dude by the collar and drug him to the back room. "Now nigga go to the back of the closet and pop the safe," the gunman ordered. The dude looked at him confused, "what you talkin bout bro?" he asked. The gunman slapped him across the face with his pistol knocking him off his feet. The gunman stood over him, "do we need to go any further with this physical abuse or will you open the safe?" he asked. The dude shook his head in cooperation and got to his feet and headed for the back of the closet with the gunman on his heels. Once the safe was open the gunman handed the dude a pillow case and made him fill it with $40,000. "Now how hard was that homey, now let's go back to the front." After the gunman and his assistant tied the three dudes up they made their way out the house. Mission Accomplished.

*   *   *

KB and Nephew was sitting outside the gambling shack mashed up, armed and dangerous. KB was furious that he allowed himself to get jipped out of $14,000 on the dice by a sharpshooting, loaded dice switching hustla. It was about 4:30 a.m. and the gambling shack was about to close. KB estimated that there were about 12 people inside including the hustla that jipped him. "Look Nephew, make sure everybody is in front of us. If a nigga act stupid you know what to do," explained KB "Aight Unk, I got you," he assured KB.

KB was Nephew's biological uncle, but they were only five years apart. KB was 28 years old and fresh off of an eight year bid for robbery. Nephew was 23 and he had finally beaten his robbery case after fighting it for four years. They came from a family of grind hard hustlas and gun slangas; both male and female, so their attitude was go get it by all means necessary.

KB led the way with two Glock Semi-Automatic .45 and Nephew followed behind him with a short black fifty round SKS. KB knocked on the door and it immediately swung open. He pressed the barrel of his glock to the big doorman's throat, "Nigga back yo bitch ass back into the shack," KB ordered. The big guy obeyed his demand and walked into the gambling area. "Hold me up phew," KB said as he stepped around the big guy and proceeded to give orders. He let off a shot into the ceiling to get everybody's attention and once he had it he went into action. "Alright, it's real simple. Everybody empty ya pockets, shoes, purses, bras, and pussies and shit will go smooth." A couple of people stalled, but the rest started getting loose, dropping knots of money on a near by table. KB sensed the ones that stalled and explained to them how dead serious he was so they needed to understand every command. He grabbed the big doorman by the back of the neck and dumped a slug into the side of his temple, splattering brain fragments everywhere. "Now for the mothafuckas that's stalling, this shit real and I just had to get out of character to make you fools understand this is not a drill. Now start getting loose or one by one, I'm gone go on a rampage," he said in a calm demeanor.

Once everybody emptied out their garments and pockets, KB pulled out a black plastic bag and filled it with the contents sitting on the pool table. "Who runs this spot?" KB asked. Nobody spoke up as they looked at each other. KB gritted his teeth and pointed his gun at the person closest to him which was a voluptuous older lady in her mid forties, she quickly pointed to the big husky man that KB recognized as the dude who jipped him. "Look out fat boy. Where the safe at?" KB asked. "It ain't no safe nigga," He answered with an extreme attitude. KB pointed and fired a slug into the big man's thigh. The big dude fell to the ground as he let out a husky growl. "Now just a little less attitude this time slick, where the safe at fat pregnant hippo built mothafucka?" KB spat. The man pointed behind the bar under the hard liquor cabinet.

Once he retrieved the code and got the money, he walked over and squatted down to the owner and whispered in his ear "You jipped the wrong nigga this time Monique Parker," KB said smiling before dumping four slugs into the fat man. He grabbed the plastic bag and headed for the front door. "You people have a nice day," he said before him and Nephew disappeared through the front door.

* * *

CHAPTER 1

BJ rolled over and grabbed his cell phone off the nightstand next to his bed and checked the ID before answering. It was his patna. "What's up KB" he asked. "Bro I know you still ain't sleep, it's 3:00 in the evening ol Hepatitis C looking ass nigga," KB said laughing into the phone. "Fuck you Louis Farrakhan," BJ shot back at him, jugging at his Muslim religion. "Oh yeah you wanna shoot at my religion huh?" Laughing through the receiver, "Alright bro you got that one, what's up?" BJ said submitting to KB's jokes.

KB and BJ hooked up when they were on the same unit together doing time. Like Nephew, BJ beat his dope and pistol case on an appeal. They clicked immediately, not only were they both bloods but they were from Dallas and knew some of the same people. So over time him, Nephew, and KB locked in and vowed to get out and get money together, by all means necessary.

"Hey dis nigga want us to meet him in about an hour to talk about this deal so get up. I'm fince to call Nephew too cause I know his retarted bird looking ass still sleep. Y'all niggas is lazy," KB said. "Aight bro,

I'm about to get ready now," BJ said before hanging up. He rolled over and kissed his main girl. She was 5'9, dark caramel beauty, with full lips, short shoulder length hair, and a tight toned body. She had nice, C-cup breasts, a flat stomach, track legs, and a nice 38 inch size butt. Some people would think that she didn't match BJ's 5'8 frame, but to them they were a perfect fit. She was his Bonnie and he was her Clyde. When he was doing his time she stayed down with him and once he got consent from his best friend, who was her brother, he immediately galed her and they have been together ever since.

"Hey boo, what's up? What time is it?" she asked, sitting up in BJ's king sized bed. "It's 3:00. I gotta go meet KB" he said, walking to the bathroom to take a shower. BJ had a nice two bedroom apartment in DeSoto, TX. It was laced with a Maroon living room set to compliment his floor to ceiling wood grain entertainment center. The kitchen was laid with marble counters and maroon cabinets to go with the rest of the house's colors. He changed the front room and made it into a dayroom with a pool table, mini wet bar, big screen T.V. with a play station 3 set, and a Sony radio with the surround sound system. BJ had been renting the apartment for about nine months and paid them an extra five thousand to add on and supersize his apartment to the size he wanted. He decked it out like a condo, overlooking DeSoto. Him and Tara didn't share apartments, they agreed to give each other their space and when time was right they would move in together. But for the time being they had separate domains and it allowed BJ the chance to stray every now and again.

When BJ got out the shower, Tara was in the kitchen washing the dishes. BJ walked behind her and kissed the nape of her neck. "What's up Boo?" Tara asked. "Hey I'm gone catch up with you tonight or tomorrow. Make sure to set the alarm and put that money on Dam-Dam books." he reminded her.

Dam-Dam was Tara's brother. Him and BJ were like brothers. They met in their early teen years in the same apartments and grew tight like a virgin's pussy. They were each other's Dame and Robby. They vowed if they left the game, they would go out just like Dame and Robby. Dame and Robby were two local bad boys that made noise in the streets. They were brothers from a different mother. They were in the dope game and Robby was set up and murdered which forced Dame to fight until his death to avenge his best friend's murder; which he successfully accomplished. Dame left behind a club in North Dallas called Robby's. It was a strip club that BJ and Dam-Dam used to visit quite often and do business with Robby's sister. BJ would still occasionally swing through and see what new foreign dancers they had.

"Still no change in Dam-Dam's case?" BJ asked as he pulled Tara into his brace. "No everything is the same; no DNA, no prints, no witness, no gun, and still no bond," she said sounding frustrated. "Don't trip baby, shit gone be good soon. They'll eventually grant his bond." he said kissing her soft lips.

Dam-Dam was in Dallas County jail fighting a bogus murder case. BJ did his best to be there for his homeboy cause he knew what it was like to be locked up. They labeled Dam-Dam a flight risk and a life risk to the victim's family and friends so they denied him

3

bond. For that reason, he's been in the county for a year now fighting the case. "Baby you be careful out there and call me when you free. I love you BJ" Tara said facing him. "I love you too," BJ said returning the love and kisses. Tara really did love BJ and it was the same on his end. They grew as friends first, then transformed into lovers. She felt protected with BJ around and they enjoyed being in each other's company. They didn't force themselves on each other; they just let things play out and if it was meant to be then they would lock each other down.

BJ hit the alarm on his midnight black box Chevy Caprice. He was rolling on some 22 inch AFC, 403; two-tone Asanti rims with the white and chrome two-tone center and matching black outing. It had plush black leather interior with the gray stitching to compliment the insides. It had Batman symbols on the seats; front and back. There were two screens in the sun visors, a lap top screen in the roof, and two in the head rest. To top it off he had two fifteens decked in hardwood with the accessories protected by plexi glass.

He hopped in and started the engine up, blasting Z-Ro's "Respect My Mind," through the speakers. He looked in the mirror and checked out his iced out grill. The top front four was decked with 14K canary yellow gold with white princess cut diamonds and a red strip. The bottom six were sold 14K canary yellow gold, with his initials on the middle two. Once he checked his grill he fired up a blunt full of white widow, he headed toward his destination. On his drive to KB's ecstasy spot in the cliff he thought about how shit had been going. It had been a year and three months since his release from TDCJ. KB kept his word and got some things in motion for him in preparation for him to come home. KB put him on his feet with a closet full of clothes and twenty-thousand to play with. BJ tried to do the 9-5 thing for a couple of months but $6.25 just wasn't cutting it for him and wasn't no good paying full time job wanting to hire an aggressive X offender. So he turned to what he knew best, the streets.

BJ pulled up to KB's spot on Kellogg off Sunnyvale and Overton. KB was sitting in the driver seat of his burnt orange round body police edition Caprice. It was filled with cocaine white guts with burnt orange stitching. He had the same inside TV accessories as BJ and his trunk was decked out with four twelve's. He was sitting on 22 inch D-93's, better know as Lorenzo's. He was accompanied by his exotic dancing X-pushing, hoe promoting hottie, Leila. She was a firm 36C-26-43, yellow bone. She favored Lisa-Raye in the face and had wavy hair that hung just above her shoulders. Today her body was complimented by a white Request halter top to show off her flat stomach and some white Request shorts to accent her thick thighs. She put the icing on the cake with her white double strapped 3 inch open toe Steve Madden heels. They showed her perfectly pedicured toes. She stood 5'9 without the heels on but with them on she stood right under KB's chin to compliment his chiseled 6'3, 195 pound frame. KB met her at Club GiGi's one night. After a couple of dreams, some nice word play, and mental penetration, she was hooked. Once he got a chance to put it down in the bedroom he was able to seal the deal. She went from being hook to being stuck. She was so strung out on KB that if he wanted her to she would strap herself up with C-4, walk into the white house and blow that bitch up. She kept it gutta though and played her role. She knew KB had a main girl and she was cool coming off the bench. They been doing their thing for about ten months and after Leila had proved herself worthy and loyal to KB, he put her in a spot with his long time homeboy Gary a*k*a Guillotine. When KB saw BJ he stood up and smiled showing his diamond clustered teeth, two at the top and six at the bottom. BJ stopped in the yard and did a quick four step, dipped his shoulders from left to right dancing to the music coming from KB's trunk. "What's up bro?" KB said as he and BJ embraced each other like they always do. "Shit feeling good," he answered. "What's up Leila?" BJ asked. "Nothing shorty, just chillin," she said as she stood up, towering over BJ's short frame giving him a hug. "How did that lick go last night?" KB asked. "Man that shit was simple as hell. Them type of niggas you can shake every six months. I told them friendly dudes that shit wasn't gone fly for long," BJ explained, while pulling out a Newport long and firing it up. "Dem niggas was in that bitch with no heat in sight. I guess they trust the suburbs too much," he said, smiling as he dapped KB up. "So what you stung foe?" KB asked. "Get out my business dawg," BJ said smiling. "We hit for forty, me and Baby Jay." "That's what's up!" KB said, smiling. "Where Nephew ol loaf of muffins built ass?" BJ asked as he blew out smoke. Just as they started riding down and cracking jokes on Nephew, he pulled up in his midnight blue Lincoln Town car. It was sitting lovely on some 22 inch, gold spinning dees. He parked behind BJ's car and hopped out followed by an entourage of smoke.

*   *   *

CHAPTER 2

"Alright this deal bro's," KB said. "I got this connect to give us a couple of them thangs but he won't give me a price. I was thinking we can start with two and see what's up." KB explained. "Ay! You know I know how to step on them hoes and get nine off both of em," BJ said, passing the blunt to Nephew. "Well shit I got two niggas right now that's looking for a couple of birds so if we get them they'll be gone that same day," Nephew said. "Sound like a deal to me," KB said, turning toward BJ. "What you think bro?" He asked. "Shit that's a bet, long as Nephew ol narcolepsy havin ass don't crawl into a corner and go to sleep on a nigga with his tired fish lookin ass," BJ said getting a laugh out of KB. "Aw nigga, you bo-legged, hog built ass be doing the same thang," Nephew said. KB stopped laughing and looked at BJ, "You do be sleeping on a nigga BJ," KB said while trying to hold his laughter in. BJ stared at both Nephew and KB, "I know what time it is. KB you just transformed into the chisel chest Auntie to save your horse stable ass niece," BJ said, laughing outrageously at his own joke.

After a couple of put downs by KB and Nephew, BJ finally submitted. They loved being in each other's company. It didn't matter what kind of situation they were in, they always added or found humor in it by cracking jokes. Through time KB found himself the thinking part of the brain, BJ was the irrational part of the brain doing dumb shit every now and again, and Nephew was the emotional, humble part of the brain. KB was the part to balance the shit and make it into an unpredictable and forceful thinking machine. They had their typical homeboy moments where an argument or disagreement would breakout but it was small things and they eventually would agree to one thing that's pleasing to them all, well two; brotherhood and money.

*　　*　　*

KB was sitting across from his new found connect, Diaz Mercardo. He controlled the drug trafficking through Dallas. He was usually discrete about dealing with black guys but he kind of owed KB a favor plus he liked his cool demeanor and how he handled things. Until this day they would occasionally run into each other at Club DMX and have a friendly drink.

They sat in a back booth at Mercardo's Caliente Mexican Restaurant to begin business. "So homey, what you trying to get?" Diaz asked, while taking a sip from his cup. "I just want to start off with two and see what's popping," KB answered. "Damn homey two? You could have went through my middle man for that," Diaz said smiling. "I don't do middle men, they always end up dead fucking with me cause at anytime they can throw shit in the game and fuck up good business relationships. So me, I deal straight up with the head nigga in charge. You feel me? That way it will never be any misunderstanding," KB said leaning back in his booth. Him and Diaz locked eyes with each other and tried to read one another. KB was secure about his game because it was simple, straight to the point, and no sugar coating. For a lot of people that was complex for them cause they didn't have that ability to be straight up. Niggas were always gamed up to get down for themselves but sometimes it was cool to let a person get down. So when shit hit the fan you can knock them off balance with your shut down defense; which was KB's way of thinking. He controlled the balance of things and never gave the chance to control to nobody. "Alright, check this out; I'm gone give you 2 for 12.5 apiece, but I'm gone front you 2 for 18.5, if not I'm gone charge you 17.5 apiece for 2," Diaz said laying his proposition out on the table. "The first one sound good but I'm gone settle with the 2 for 17.5 each," KB said sounding secure about his option. He didn't want to be reliable for another nigga's dope, nor did he want to accept and seem desperate. "Are you sure homey?" Diaz asked. "Yeah I don't lay right with handouts. I'm good with working my way to the top, ya feel me. I appreciate the offer though. No disrespect intended," KB said. "None taken homey," Diaz said.

KB walked outside to his care to retrieve the money. He made a motion with his hand to indicate to BJ and Nephew things were straight. They were ducked off across the street in a non suspicious car on standby in case KB needed back up if things didn't go right. KB took Diaz the cash and soon as they made the swap KB was back in his car heading to his next destination

*   *   *

"Man, why you didn't jump on that deal?" BJ asked KB while sitting at the domino table across from him. "Cause bro, I want that fool to respect our hustle. When he see that we runnin through these hoes he won't have no choice but to chop our shit to 12.5, no front," KB explained. "That's what's up bro," BJ said, agreeing with his motive. Nephew walked out the back room flipping his cell phone shut. "Hey these niggas done renigged on the deal," he said. "He just wanted half so I stung his ass for 11.5, fuck it he a hoe anyway. Just give me a week with the other half and it'll be gone. I'm gone let Kayla do her thang," Nephew explained.

Kayla was Nephew's main girl. She was a black and Puerto Rican beauty about 5'3, 125 pounds. Her body frame reminded you of Megan Good. She had smooth golden skin, long wavy hair, green eyes and a baby face. She was the manager at her brother's five figures a week strip club called Connections. It was the spot for the city's high rollers and ballers.

Later on that night BJ got the supplies he needed to step on the birds. He broke the first one down and got 9 ounces out of it. He put the rest of the bird on a flat cooking pan and added the blow up to it. He added about 254.7 grams worth of blow up to the bird. After he mixed the blow up in with the bird, he laid out three sheets of saran wrap and dumped the contents on it. He proceeded to wrap it thoroughly. Once it was wrapped tight he placed the bird in between two pieces of plywood to get into brick form. Then he placed a piece of wood over the top of it and lightly stepped on it to knock the air out it and compress it back into a block. After he finished, he did the other the same way. When his mission was complete he threw both the birds on the table in front of Nephew and KB. "There it is. Let em sit until tomorrow," BJ said, firing up half a dro blunt. "I got this esse I fuck with gone get this 9 for 8.5. We winning on a couple of G's so that's what's up," he said inhaling a cloud of smoke. "Shit, at this rate we ought to be able to double our shot without a major break down on some rock for rock shit," BJ said. "Most likely we'll make about an eleven or twelve thousand dollar apiece profit so that's what's up," KB said, puffing on the dro blunt.

*   *   *

It took the trio about four or five days to get off everything they had. They were at KB's spot off Skillman. He had a nice two bedroom, two bath refurnished spot. KB chose to stay in North Dallas because it was low key but at the same time it has some balanced action. They were looking at an even sixty-two thousand, they split the profit and KB kept the thirty-six to re-up. "Shit if we can keep rocking like this, we won't have to extort those hoe ass niggas," BJ said, putting rubber bands around his three stacks of money. BJ really wasn't the jacking type; he was more into the numbers game. KB and Nephew were born jackers. If they didn't feel like the person with it should have it, then they would take it with no hesitation. A quick valuable lick was always necessary for KB and

Nephew and it was rubbing off on BJ cause he was with whatever they were with.

KB left the table to go entertain his main squeeze Stacy. She was a sexy paper sack brown Caribbean beauty. She was from the Virgin Islands but moved to Dallas when she was sixteen. She had beautiful jet black, long hair that complimented her erotic facial features. She had greenish slanted Chinese eyes, a sharp jaw structure, and some full brown luscious lips. She stood 5'2, with a 34C-24-40 measurement and to seal the deal she had a slight dip in the bottom of her back to make her ass look like the perfect heart shape. Stacy was KB's balance. It wasn't anything she wouldn't do for him and vice versa. She was the outgoing laid back, down for whatever type chic. She was into urban modeling and had recently dubbed the digital dime piece of her MySpace page. She was a good girl with a good head on her shoulders and she knew how to get down and nasty for her man in the bedroom.

"Hey!" KB yelled from the backroom. "You two doughboys gone and burn off, I'm fince to give baby some Q.T." he said laughing. "Fuck that!" You always tryin to run a nigga off. I need some us time too," Nephew said. "Come on bro." KB said in a squeaky voice. "I ain't with that punk shit. I like short curvaceous females, not tall faded up studs. Man you and BJ get y'all hoe asses outta my house," KB said laughing. BJ and Nephew voted against starting a scoring marathon cause it always ended up with KB being the aggressor, so they exited and went their separate ways.

* * *

CHAPTER 3

BJ was riding around Cedar Hill looking to run into Bowie. He was an old associate that BJ used to chill and smoke weed with. Well times were different and Bowie was one of the reasons Dam-Dam was still locked up. He agreed with the D.A. to testify against Dam-Dam to get his dope cases dropped. He was what they called a character witness.

As he was driving up Weaver St. he saw the female that he used to knock down in high school. She was strutting up the street with a little girl walking in front of her. She was rocking some white Prada shorts, a matching white sleeveless top, and some icy white low top Nike forces. Her hair was braided and her tummy cut shirt revealed a tribal tattoo that wrapped around her stomach. He pulled into the duplex and hopped out. "Look out Lisa," he yelled from across the street. She stopped and squinted her eyes trying to see who was calling her. After she saw who it was she put her hand over her mouth as if she was surprised. He made his way across the street. Lisa was a bad little bo-legged yellow bone. She had Philippine facial features, nice Tisha Campbell lips, a handful of teeny bopper breasts, and a small apple bottom butt that fit perfect with her 5'5 frame. "Oh my God BJ!" she said running and jumping in his arms. "It's been six years since I've seen you," she said, kissing his cheek. "I know, what's been up?" BJ said smiling showing his diamond flooded grill. "I've been doing good, going to school," she replied. "Is that your little girl?" "Yeah! Come here Lizzarha." The little girl walked over and grabbed her mother's hand. "Say hello to my friend BJ," Lisa said smiling from ear to ear. BJ squatted to the little girl's level and stuck his hand out. "Hey Lizzarha, that's a pretty name for a pretty girl," he said smiling. "Thank you Mr. BJ," she said in a shy manner. "Just call me BJ, fuck that mr shit. How old are you?" BJ asked. "I just turned 4 yesterday," she answered. BJ pulled out a wad of money and pulled off a twenty, "here you go, happy late birthday," BJ said. "Thank you," she said smiling. He stood back up and faced Lisa. He looked into her deep seductive gray eyes. That was the thing he used to love about her the most. When they used to sex each other back in the day, he would like to do it with the lights on so he could look into her exotic eyes. "Damn man, it's been a minute," BJ said, licking his lips. "I know right," she answered, feeling like a school girl all over again. "Well say I gotta bounce you gotta numba so we can stay in touch," he said, pulling out his red razor thin Sprint phone.

After they exchanged numbers they parted ways. BJ didn't know it but Lisa was instantly digging him all over again. Not only was his appearance still appealing, but he had a throwed swagger; money and a nice car. She wondered if his sex game was still on point. Back when they were in high school they were inseparable. Lisa stayed directly in the duplex behind

BJ's and in the middle of the night he would sneak through her window and they would sex each other until the roosters croaked, non-stop. After school he would walk her home and they would have a sex marathon until her mother arrived.

She stood there and watched BJ cruise down the street and out of sight. Her thoughts of their past made her want him all over again.

*   *   *

BJ pulled up in the Exxon on the corner of Beltline. Just as he was walking in, Bowie was walking out. It had been some years since they've seen each other but Bowie knew how close Dam-Dam and BJ were. The last he heard on BJ was that he had 25 years and wasn't due for parole until 2017. Here it was 2007 and he was staring in the eyes of the tiger. He was nervous but he still played it cool.

"What's up BJ?" he spoke. Bowie stood well over BJ at 6'2 and he had a solid build but he knew BJ's rep so it wasn't in him to try him. BJ smiled before he spoke, "I guess you niggas out here thought I wouldn't touch down no time soon huh?" BJ said now staring in Bowie's eyes. "Ain't no words needed nigga, just know that I'm in the streets and shit gone get real stupid," he said as he walked passed Bowie into the store to pay for his gas. BJ was careful not to talk reckless but enough to make the nigga feel him. Bowie was close to the nigga that Dam-Dam supposedly killed but instead of holding court in the streets, niggas was running to the laws but BJ was determined to get his nigga from behind that glass by all means necessary.

*   *   *

Nephew was parked outside his supposed to be baby mama, Lina's, apartments. She had been claiming he was the daddy before he got locked up. Nephew had doubts about him being the father but he went with the flow until he ran into the other dude that she was messing around with at the same time he was knocking her down. Nephew coincidently ran into him while they were on the same unit and once Nephew saw him and chopped it up with him, his doubt was confirmed. Now he was going through the drama of getting a blood test. Lina was absolutely not trying to get a blood test. She argued that she was sure who the baby daddy was and a D.N.A. test was not needed but Nephew was determined to make it happen. Lately he had been having words with her boyfriend, Lonzo. Nephew had no tithes to Lina emotionally, mentally, or spiritually but sexually he felt like he had tithes to letting her suck him up every now and again cause the head was beyond great.

He hopped out the car and made his way to her apartment. Lina still stayed with her mother. She was the oldest of her brother and sister at 20. She had absolutely nothing going for herself. Her sister, Me'Ona, had a job, no kids, and she was going to TWU in Denton majoring in Business. Her little brother was a whole nother story. Nephew knocked on the door as he leaned his 6'1, cut frame against it. Nephew had been up all night running pounds, smoking weed, and drinking. He only got three hours of sleep so he was in a grumpy ass mood and didn't feel like going through no drama with Lina. Lina answered the door in a white see through lingerie tank top and some white silk boy shorts. They stared each other down and Nephew ran his eyes up and down her body. She was a 5'4, peanut butter brown skin hood beauty. She was a simple 32C-24-36. Nephew was attracted to her body but he was drawn to her Egyptian lips and head service. Once he surveyed her body without showing any signs of play, he walked past her into the house and sat on the couch. For once, the place was spotless. Lina walked into the living room and un-paused the radio and continued doing what she was doing. She walked into the kitchen and went back to cooking. Nephew laid on the couch and tried to erase the sexual images from his mind. He got up from the couch and went where his nose led him; to the kitchen where Lina was frying some chicken, french fries, mac-n-cheese, and good ol sweet rice. Lina was dancing around the kitchen to Mariah Carey's, Touch My Body, as she cooked and sipped on a Smirnoff.

"Damn that smell good," Nephew said rubbing his stomach. "You could have spoke when you walked by me," she said. "I spoke with my eyes, what did you expect a hug and kiss. You know we don't rock like that. I wouldn't want your boyfriend to freak out," he said sarcastically. "Fuck you Marco," she said, calling him by his real name. "You don't say that when I got my lips wrapped around yo shit," she said rolling her eyes. "You do that by choice," Nephew said, chuckling a little bit. "Look at you. You drinking, cooking, and walking around in these skimpy clothes. You make a nigga want some head," he said shaking his head. "Whatever nigga," she said flicking her wrist, turning off the burner on the stove. "You can make your plate if you want to" she said. "You might as well make mine and yours, don't be like that Lina," Nephew said, walking back into the living room. "Punk you think you slick" Lina yelled out. "Naw, you think you slick running around with that shit on," Nephew yelled from the living room.

The phone rung and Nephew picked it up, "Hello" he answered. "Say man put Lina on the phone," The male voice demanded. "Hold up bro, I know that's your chic but don't call like you checkin a nigga," Nephew said into the phone.

It was Lina's boyfriend, Lonzo. Him and Nephew squared off before and Nephew got the best of him behind Lonzo acting stiff. Lonzo was a small time dope boy in North Dallas. He pushed quarter birds and had a weed spot in Stoney Brook Apartments. He had a small crew that he ran with but they were all peons that only a selective few respected in the streets. "Nigga why you ansin my bitch phone anyway?" Lonzo barked. "You know what time it is pimp. Don't play dumb," Nephew giggled in the phone. "Just calm down when you call," Nephew said dropping the phone. "Lina yo shawty on the phone," Nephew said. Lina walked in the living room and handed Nephew his plate. "Why you be doing that" she asked frowning. "Just tell dude to calm down. I don't want you, that's old news," Nephew said biting into his chicken. "Fuck you nigga," Lina said grabbing the phone. "Hello," she answered. "Hey you gone get that fool popped. If he keep disrespecting my G," Lonzo barked into the phone. "OK Lonzo damn stop yelling," she said. "Naw bitch cause you don't seem to get what a nigga saying. I know that's yo baby daddy and I know you a hot girl, but I ain't no hoe and dude gone understand what I'm saying," Lonzo said, obviously very bitter. "OK baby," Lina said submissively.

After she had her brief conversation with Lonzo she proceeded to finish her food. "Marco, why don't you give my nigga a break?" she asked. "That nigga thank fat meat ain't greasy, all he had to do was ask to speak to you the right way and I wouldn't have said shit. But since he wanna act stiff, that's how he gone end up so don't talk to me. Holla at ya boy," Nephew said.

After they ate Lina proceeded with her plans to seduce Nephew. She crawled in his lap and tried to give him a lap dance. Nephew played along, then denied her access. He was reluctant to fuck Lina cause he wanted her to know he had power, but he also know she wasn't worth the drama. "Please Marco, fuck me!" she begged as she unbuckled his shorts and massaged his snake. She pulled it out and dropped her head in his lap and did what she did best. Nephew did what he did best and enjoyed some of the best head ever gotten until he came in her mouth.

*   *   *

CHAPTER 4

KB, Guillotine, Nephew, and BJ was headed to a party in Pleasant Grove to confront a local jack boy named Snooky. He was putting out the word that his jack crew was hot and KB and his peeps were on the top of his hit list. Snooky was a coward with a gun and if push came to shove he would shoot. Around his area it was a few that barred him because he was known to get reckless but he played a dirty and shisty game and it was a lot that didn't care for his presence.

KB pulled up in front of a brown brick house off of Buckner. He knew the dude throwing the party and when he pulled up he saw a couple of familiar faces but he still approached the situation with his gun cocked and his crew ready. When they stepped out the car, the front yard only had a handful of males and females mingling and drinking. They heard the music bumping and headed for the inside. It was flooded with females in tight small clothing, bopped up and shaking their ass. It was a few dudes holding up the wall, drinking up the drank and a couple more dudes indulging in some hood jiggin. KB and his crew laid low and peeped the scenery. Nephew and BJ chatted with a few of the girls but KB and Guillotine were ducked off by the front door, watching and stalking the crowd.

"Hey bro go get BJ and Nephew and meet me by the back door," KB whispered in Guillotine's ear. Guillotine proceeded to gather up the two playboys and headed to the spot. While KB was waiting for them P-Man walked through the door. "What's up bro," P-Man asked sticking his hand out for some dap. "What's up bro," KB answered. "How long you been here?" "About twenty minutes." "I ain't seen you in a while. Where ya boys at?" P-Man asked, knowing they were somewhere close. "They around here somewhere," KB said standing firm and motionless. P-Man detected something was up but he didn't want to stress it. "Hey I'm gone catch up with ya later, Y'all be cool, huh." "Bet" KB said.

Right as P-Man walked in one direction, Guillotine, BJ, and Nephew came from another and they all stepped in the back yard. It was full of people but KB was still able to spot Snooky in the corner with two niggas from his crew, Bren and Creep. Creep was the muscle and been Snooky's right hand. Creep was about 6'1, solid jet black and solid muscle. Bren was about 5'8, paper sack brown and thin in the wind and was known as a hot head. KB told BJ and Nephew to go stand under both lights after Snooky and his boys spotted KB. Him and Guillotine made their way through the crowd of people. KB could see Snooky but Snooky couldn't see him. Snooky stood up to try to spot KB but was unsuccessful. He looked to both corners and saw BJ and Nephew in their spots. He knew something was about to jump off so he alarmed his partners and then reached for his pistol.

"That's not necessary," a voice spoke from behind him. He froze, and then turned around only to be faced off with KB and Guillotine. He looked down and saw that Guillotine had a black glock in his hand held by his side. "What's yo purpose," Snooky asked. "I don't know, tell me; what was yo purpose for thinking you had to draw down on us?" KB asked. "Nigga, I'm just being cautious," he said. "Naw," KB said shaking his head. "You know what's up. I just came to tell you to think about yo moves before you make them. Me or my crew is not to be fucked with," he said with confidence. "And what makes you niggas untouchable," Bren barked. "I do," KB said pointing to himself. "And who the fuck is you?" Bren said. By now people were at attention listening to the conflict taking place but KB wasn't worried cause he had BJ and Nephew strapped in both corners of the back yard and him and Guillotine were strapped like seat belts. "I'm gone dismiss you for right now cause you don't know no betta," KB said pointing to his brain. "All I'm saying to you Snooky is don't red light ya life." Bren stepped up closer to KB challenging him to spit box, but again KB dismissed him and walked passed him. "That's what I'm saying hoe nigga, you don't make no calls around the Grove," he barked. KB turned and faced him, the next thing you heard was KB's long left hook connecting with Bren's jaw making him stagger a bit. KB then followed with a stiff right-left jab dropping him and drawing blood from his nose and mouth. Creep wanted to make a move but was stuck cause Guillotine had him at point blank so he let things play out. Snooky walked over and helped his right hand stand up. At first he staggered then he held his balance. "I'm through talking," KB said. "If shit ain't clear then it will be in the end," he said calmly as him and Guillotine walked toward the back door. KB and his crew stood together on the back porch and watched as people went back to having a good time, and then made their exit.

*   *   *

BJ was sitting in the living room bagging up ounces and smoking on a blunt when his cell phone started playing UGK's, Take It Off, ringtone. He looked at the caller ID and checked to see if Tara was still in the shower before answering. "Hello." "Is this BJ?" the female voice asked. "Yeah, what's up with it Lisa?" "You're not busy are you?" she asked.

Her and BJ had been talking faithfully every other day for the past two weeks since they ran into each other. He played his cards right so he wouldn't get jammed up with Tara. "A lil bit but what's up?" he asked. "Do you got plans for the weekend?" she asked sounding seductive. "Naw, why? You wanna hook up?" he asked smiling. "Yeah if you free. I got a itch that needs to be scratched, you think you can handle that?" she asked. "What! Fucking right I can handle that. Just keep that thang on ice for me," he said happily. "It's a date then," she agreed. "Bet," BJ said before hanging up the phone.

"Keep what on ice?" Tara asked from behind him startling him. "Oh shit! You sced the hell out of me Tara," he said trying to buy him some time to make up a quick lie. "What you keeping on ice?" she asked again, drying off her hair. "Oh that was KB, he just bought me a pint of drank so I told him to keep it on ice till I got there," he said standing up wrapping his arms around her, gripping a handful of ass. "mmmmph . . ." she said. "So what you want to eat tonight?" she asked as she walked into the kitchen. He immediately got lost in a daze as he stared at her perfectly shaped body. BJ loved making love to Tara. Not only did she look like ebony eye candy, but she tasted like it. He loved the power that he had to make her cum repeatedly. It took him a quick minute to master the skill of oral pleasure but he finally got it down packed thanks to Nephew. Nephew would always remind BJ of the power that the tongue possessed. He would encourage BJ to give his girl a bashful tongue lasting and it would all work out in his favor. Not only did Tara enjoy the lasting but she stepped her game up on the Fellatio blast also. "Gone head and hook up some chicken fried steak" he said snapping out of his last filled day dream. He finished bagging up his ounces and him and Tara ate.

While he was putting dishes in the dishwasher his cell phone went off. "Hello" "Say bro, I need you to come through my spot in the Cliff, it's an emergency," KB said. "Alright, I'm on my way" He hung up the phone and walked into the dining area where Tara was sitting with a frown on her face. "Where you going? I thought we were gonna chill tonight?" she asked. Tara wasn't the bug-a-boo nagging type but she loved being in BJ's company and lately their time has been short. "KB need me at the spot," he said holding her in his arms. "But you didn't have dessert," she said in a playful whining voice. "Come here boo," BJ said leading her to the big marble covered, wooden table. He sat her on the table and kissed her soft luscious lips passionately. He slipped her booty shorts off and massaged her perfectly bald shaved chocolate pudding pop. She was moist and her juices were running down her thighs as BJ played with her G-spot. She leaned back and braced herself on the table, then threw her head back as BJ worked her clit with his thumb. "I know I've been running dem streets lately, but you stay on my mind," he whispered in her ear as she held her breath and enjoyed the pleasure. BJ knelt down and slowly licked the juices off her thigh. He made his way to her dripping middle and softly sucked on her swollen lips. Tara moaned out loud as BJ worked his finger around her cave. He licked and sucked on her pearl as he slid his finger in and out of her opening. "Mmmm . . . . baby," she moaned as she gripped his head. She laid all the way back on the table and arched her back as he stuck his tongue in her hole and twirled it in circles with his thumb working her sensitive clit. Tara could barely hold her composure as she let out a few loud cries; "Ohhh . . . BJ," she said before locking up and having an explosive orgasm.

BJ went to the back and fixed himself up as Tara tried to come down off cloud nine. She climbed off the table and smiled as if she could still feel BJ's tongue tickling her insides. "Damn dat nigga a fool," she said to herself as she cleaned the dining table.

*   *   *

BJ pulled up to KB's spot off Sunnyvale and noticed more cars than usual. He hopped out and headed for the door. "Come on in," KB yelled from the inside. BJ walked in and greeted everybody in the living room. Between BJ, Nephew, and KB, they all had a crew outside of each other that backed them up on trying to build and empire. BJ had a team of five called the dream team. They were from different parts of Dallas but had migrated to Cedar Hill. They stayed on the same street as BJ's mother which is how he befriended them. J-Note was from South Dallas and was around KB's age, 28. Jeff was J-Notes cousin; they were what you would consider the muscle of the crew. J-Note has a crew of young niggas under him that were destined to prove themselves. Then it was Velt, George, and Bam. They were all from East Dallas. BJ had known them for the longest. George and Bam were brothers and Velt was their brother from another mother. Nephew had a team of two gun slangers, LD and Marcus. Nephew and LD basically built Marcus into a human robot. Nephew was closer to LD but he still was loyal to all of his boys and showed them the same love. As far as KB, he had his main man, Guillotine. Guillotine was hands down, ride or die no doubt.

BJ copped a seat on the couch as KB proceeded to feel him in on the problem at hand. "So what's the dillyo bro?" BJ asked as he fired up a Newport long. "Baby Jay got downed last night bro. and they also hit him for half a brick so we took two losses in one night," he said looking around the room. "That was ya boy BJ so I know you gone want the jump on this," KB said. BJ sat back and let the information soak in. Baby Jay was BJ's lil homey from the same hood. Baby Jay did five years at T.Y.C. and was released when he turned eighteen. Him and BJ would hit licks together, fuck bitches, and get money. When Baby Jay's grandmother died, BJ helped him back on his feet by putting him in an apartment. He included Baby Jay in everything he did and now he was gone. "Damn bro," BJ said rubbing his head. "You got any info on what happened?" he asked. "All I know is that two niggas jammed him up going in his spot, robbed him and popped him," KB explained. BJ sat in a daze for a minute. He stood up and headed for the front door. "Hold up bro, where you going?" KB asked. "I got some shit to handle bro," BJ said as he walked out the door and headed for his car. Nephew proceeded to stop BJ but KB halted Nephew in his tracks. "Man you know that fool bound to do some crazy shit," Nephew said looking at his uncle, then at BJ pulling away from the curb. "He'll be aight. Let him blow off some steam, fuck some shit up," KB said.

They all knew BJ was all action. He did the first thing that came to his mind. If he was pressured by KB to think first things would come out for the better but if he didn't think first then shit would end up in chaos. But that was how BJ operated and KB knew he had enough street smarts to handle himself in situations

*   *   *

BJ pulled up in some apartments known as "The Browns" in Highland Hills. That's where Baby Jay had a spot and BJ wasn't too fond of the spot because he knew how those dudes rolled in that area. Baby Jay assured him that his cousin, Black Mike, would make sure he was straight over there. Black Mike was well known around the entire Highland Hills area and he helped Baby Jay set up in the browns so he could make some money. Some of the dudes over time wasn't down with the idea of an unknown hustler, but due to Black

Mike's reputation nobody questioned it. Things were all good until Mike got ten years FED for getting busted with half a brick, two AK's, and $40,000 in cash. Local dope boy, Profit, felt like it was time to move Baby Jay around so they occasionally bumped heads. BJ made his presence known in the browns by befriending a couple of the small time hustlas over there with small favors. He was also fucking the baddest chic over there so some of the dudes let him room. The ones under Profit didn't take too highly of his presence but they knew Black Mike wouldn't be locked up forever.

BJ pulled up in the browns and headed straight to the back. He pulled up in front of Baby Jay's old complex and walked in the opposite direction towards one of Profit's spots. He went up the stairs and knocked on the door. "Who is it?" a voice yelled from behind the door. "Look through the peep hole nigga," BJ answered. After about thirty seconds the door swung open and a skinny black dude with braids stood in the doorway. "What's your business?" he asked. "Barry you know why I'm here. Where's Profit?" BJ said, holding his mug. "Profit ain't got no words for you," Barry barked. BJ pulled out two pistols and put them in Barry's face, "back yo bitch ass in the apartment," BJ commanded. With his hands in the air Barry backed into the apartment and they walked into the living room where Profit was sitting on a couch counting money. He was accompanied by two men that BJ recognized as Flip and Dooley. Once they saw what was going down they immediately reached for their pistols. BJ pointed one of the pistols at Profit as the other one stayed on Barry. "I don't think grabbing them guns gone do nobody no justice cause I'll set this bitch off," BJ said. Profit motioned for his boys to chill and proceeded to find out what his beef was. "Sit yo bitch ass down Barry," BJ spat. Barry stood his position and didn't move, staring BJ down. BJ stepped up and caught Barry across the side of the head, dropping him. "Now sit yo weak ass down before it be two funerals this weekend," BJ said. He turned his attention to Profit and they held each other's gaze for a few seconds. "What's your reason BJ?" Profit asked in a cool manner. "Don't play me Profit man. My nigga dead and right now you suspect nigga," BJ said gripping his pistols. "So you barge in my spot with yo guns out making demands?" Profit asked in an agitated tone. "Put them guns up and we can have a civilized conversation," Profit said. "Nigga fuck that, I'm the judge and I'm holding court right now. Now tell me what the fuck I want to hear and now or I'm gone paint this apartment with brain fragments," BJ said holding his ground. "Oh so you on a crash mission huh?" Profit asked. "Naw if I was on a crash mission I would have came through that door squeezing this trigger. Now tell me what the fuck happened to Baby Jay." Profit shrugged, "all I know is that somebody followed the nigga home, got him in the house, and you know the rest," he said sarcastically. "So what makes you exempt from all this? I know you coward ass niggas didn't want him over here. So convince me you didn't set him up," BJ said. "Look you can take my yes for a yes and my no for a no and draw your own conclusion. If I would have had something to do with it, I would have hit him, Big Mike, and his crew all at one time. But I wasn't losing out on no major money while Baby J was here so he was no big deal," Profit explained as he picked up a pack of Newports off the table, slid one out and fired it up. "Fuck man!" BJ yelled. "I swear Profit, I don't barr you or your crew and it I find out otherwise you had something to do with Baby Jay getting killed, you better be ready cause I'm coming from all four corners," BJ said, backing toward the doorway. "I hope you a man of your word," Profit said as BJ made his way out the apartment. "Tell the crew what the business is and if you ever in a position to jump on that fool, get rid of him," Profit explained to his crew.

He knew of BJ's reputation and attitude so Profit knew it was in his best interest to get the jump on him because BJ was unpredictable. Profit admired his courage though because he didn't know anybody that was bold enough to run in his spot with their guns out, wreck havoc, and let them live. He definitely had a hot head on his hands and those could be bad for your health.

*   *   *

CHAPTER 5

It was two days into spring break and LD took a small lost. Nephew gave him a half of brick to get rid of and on his way to the drop, the laws rolled him. He did what he did best and ran while dumping the dope out in the Trinity River that ran behind Bonton Projects in South Dallas. Somehow he didn't make it out of the law's four block radius and they caught him. He was charged with fleeing the scene. Nephew bonded him out and now they were posted up outside Club Tropical in North Dallas. Nephew was messing with one of the females that worked in the club. She had been sexing the owner until a pretty Cuban girl with an exotic body and foreign head started stripping there. The owner started mistreating her and using her so she was anxious to make him pay.

"Alright this is the lay out. Bay got two pistols ready for us in the last stall in the bathroom," Nephew said as he puffed on a tightly rolled sweet. "At 12:15 the guard that guards the stairs does a perimeter check so we will have about ten minutes to make our move. You ready?" Nephew asked. "Yeah let's do this LD said, dapping Nephew up.

Once they got patted down at the door they headed for the bar. Nephew scanned the strip club full of half naked tropical females but he didn't see Bay anywhere. Him and LD ordered a couple shots of Patron before he heard a sexy voice behind him, "Hey sexy! What's up?" Bay said in a soft sensual tone. Nephew turned around and checked out the half Cuban, half Philippine beauty. Bay was about 5'10 with a brown sugar complexion. She was a firm 32D-26-42 and everything about Bay turned you on from her slanted eyes to her lips, down to her soft touch. She was an exotic woman with good charisma and she loved everything about Nephew. Even though she stripped for a living, he respected her and whenever she needed him or needed something, he did what he could do for her. She accepted the fact that he would never love her or gal her but she loved being in Nephew's presence and the sex was good.

"What's up Bay baby?" Nephew said kissing her cheek. "Everything you ask for is in the stall," she said whispering in his ear. "I'll catch up with you later daddy. You two be careful," she said before walking off. Nephew and LD went to the bathroom and just like Bay said, everything was there; two guns and two masks. After they strapped up they made their way back to the back of the club. From a distance Nephew watched the guard that stood under an off limit sign. The guard checked his watch and just like Bay said he looked around and walked towards the front of the club. Nephew and LD made their way to the door as they put their masks on and headed up stairs. Nephew put his ear to the door and heard the click of a money machine going. He looked at LD and LD put his foot through the door knocking it smooth off the hinge. The owner, a tall white man in his mid thirties, was totally caught off guard so they had the jump on him.

"Look this shit is real simple. We put the money in the bag and make our exit and nobody gets hurt," Nephew barked. "This is some bullshit. You can't rob me," the white man said. "Shut up and get on the ground," Nephew said. LD proceeded to put the money from the machine in his bag and then grabbed the stacks out of the safe that was already open. "It's clean," LD said. "Stand up," Nephew ordered the man. The man stood up and Nephew caught him in the back of the head with the gun knocking him cold out. Once they got what they wanted and the coast was clear, they headed for the exit; Mission accomplished.

*   *   *

Nephew laid on his back as the tingling sensation rushed through his body. Bay softly sucked on the head of Nephew's dick like a Popsicle as she stroked his shaft. She then ran her tongue slowly down the back of his piece reaching his nuts. As she continued to lick both of them she screw balled his dick with two fingers. Bay put one nut in her mouth and gently sucked on it as if she was sucking on a watermelon jolly rancher. "Mmmm . . . . damn Bay, you doing yo thang," Nephew said, looking down smiling as she made her way back to his dick. This time she wasted no time deep throating him. Once she had him in her mouth she used the back of her throat to gently suck as she applied pressure with her jaws and the roof of her mouth. She sucked and sucked, slurped and slurped, until Nephew begged her to stop. "Turn over and arch your back for me," Nephew said. Once Bay was in position, Nephew rubbed her slit with the tip of his head to tease her. "Don't do me like that baby," Bay said seductively. Nephew slowly slid all of his manhood into her dripping tight, wet pussy. She let out soft moans as Nephew filled every inch of her vagina. As he dropped off in her hole like an anchor, he reached under her and massaged her clitoris. "Mmmm . . . sssss . . . fuck! That feels good," Bay said as she buried her head in the sheets. "You like that?" Nephew asked as he banged her insides at a slow pace. "I wanna ride that dick," she said. Nephew grabbed her waist and they ended up in the reverse cowboy position. Bay leaned forward and grabbed Nephew's ankles as she bounced up and down slowly on his dick. "Yeahhhh . . . do that shit," Nephew said while rubbing her soft ass and licking his lips as he watched his dick go in and out her pretty pink pussy. Bay sat straight up on his dick and let every inch fill her as she moved her hips in circular motion. "Ooooh . . . . Nephew," she moaned as he worked her spot. She turned to face him and Nephew helmed her up missionary style. She held her legs up as Nephew balanced himself and miraculously smashed her insides until he reached his peak. He pulled out and exploded all over the face of her pussy.

* * *

"Man there go that nigga KB," Creep said as they rode over M.L.K. KB was parked at a carwash on M.L.K. but what they didn't know was that KB was across the street at a raided shop dropping off nine ounces to one of his people from X-Line, also known as 44 Oakland. Bren reached in the back of the SUV and retrieved a 30 shot Tech-9 from under the back seat. "Look swang right where we'll come from the passenger side. I'll be able to spray the whole car from that angle," Bren explained.

It was a caramel skin female standing outside the car talking to somebody through the window so they knew somebody was in the car. "What about that broad?" Creep asked. "Fuck it, she in the wrong place, wrong time. Now drive slow," Bren ordered. They approached their target from about thirty feet and Bren hung out the passenger side of the SUV and sprayed and entourage of bullets at his foe, *[Platt . . . platt . . . . tat . . . tat . . . tat . . . tat . . . tat . . . . tat . . . tat . . .]*. Once his clip was empty and he was satisfied with his attack, Creep made a left on MLK and made their get a way.

KB ran out the shop with his gun in his hand toward his car. The first thing he saw was a pretty brown skin girl lying in glass in her own blood and lifeless with a body full of bullets. He turned his attention towards his bullet riddled car and proceeded to open the passenger side door. When he did, his partner, Dough fell into his arms spitting up blood trying to fight for his life. KB sat on the ground with Dough in his lap. "Come on bro, you gotta fight this," KB said rocking his longtime friend back and forth in his arms.

Dough was part of KB's Hot Boy crew back when they were in high school. Dough was one of the many who stayed in touch with KB through his trials and tribulations. He had just cut some tracks with local rappers, Mr. Pookie and Lucci and was trying to make that transition from the streets to the booth so he could focus on his career. But reality made him face the facts that he still had to eat.

KB held Dough as he slowly slipped into death. Blood continued to run from the corners of his mouth as his breathing slowed. KB faced reality and accepted the fact that Dough wouldn't make it but he continued to hold him. "Just breathe easy bro. I got you. Believe that," KB said as the rage inside of him boiled. Dough took his last breath then his body went limp. KB closed Dough eyes just as the paramedics and police arrived on the scene. By then a small crowd had formed around the scene and the police went straight to work asking questions while the paramedics rolled the two corpses to the ambulance. Two detectives drilled KB but got nothing out of him. KB knew how to hold his ground with the police and he abided by the G-code and that was to hold court in the streets.

*   *   *

CHAPTER 6

KB sat in a black lazy boy posted up in the living room. He sat in the dark and looked out his patio door at the Dallas Skyline. He puffed on a blunt as he thought over and over about how he would fulfill his revenge. After his own investigation, his theory was proven about Snooky having something to do with Dough getting killed. The day after Dough boy was killed, KB decided to put his trap on Snooky. Wild Cherry was one of KB's goldmines and she was indeed a true trap. Standing at 5'5 and 140 solid pounds, she was a Brazilian and Dominican beauty. She had reddish brown skin and long curly, water wavy, light brown hair that hung to the mid of her back. She reminded KB of a light brown, young Angel Conwell. When she came to KB she was very submissive. She always went out of her way to make sure KB was satisfied no matter what the case was. She was loyal to KB and would jump off a bridge if he asked her to.

KB found out that Snooky was a young trick daddy and didn't mind paying for what he wanted. With the right amount of liquor in his system, some bomb weed, and off the chain head, he was bound to tell it all. He would be willing to spill his guts to the president. Every time he was in the company of Wild Cherry, he felt comfortable enough to give up valuable information and just like the good girl she was, she reported all of the info back to KB.

Wild Cherry stood in front of KB butt naked, dripping water. KB stared at her silhouette as it shined from the moonlight. His eyes went straight to her perfectly shaved kitten. Wild Cherry slowly rubbed her glistening body as her and KB locked eyes. Her right hand tickled her left nipple as her left hand slid back and forth between her wet slit. KB licked his lips as his manhood poked between the hole of his boxers. He slid them off and slowly stroked his piece. Wild Cherry loved the way that KB filled her cave with his massive third leg. She walked over to the chair and climbed into KB's lap. She held her breath as she positioned herself to receive him. KB slid a little bit of dick into her warm flesh as she slowly worked her hips. He held her butt cheeks while she braced to receive the rest of his nine and a half inches. She let out soft moans as she slowly bounced on his dick. "Ssss . . . damn this shit feel good," she said working her hips in a circular motion. KB felt her juices drip down his leg as she rode him like a Harley. "Mmmm . . . baby . . . . I got the last piece of info you needed," she said softly in his ear. KB licked her ear, "what is it?" he asked. "Snooky and his bitch gone make a move on this nigga named Cliff on Saturday for two birds and some money," she said moaning. "What's the lay out?" he said moving his hips in rhythm with hers. "ooohh . . . shit . . . the dude Cliff suppose to meet up with Snooky's bitch before he drop the dope and money and that's when

Snooky gone make his move," Wild Cherry said as she arched her back and grinded hard on his dick. "Where?" he asked. "In Red Bird at Motel 6 behind Deny's, 10:30 p.m," she said as she worked his dick. "Good girl," he said. He bent her over the arm of the chair and pleased her with some deep penetration. She cried and moaned, gripping and clinching the couch as she felt herself about to climax. "Ssss . . . I'm bout to cum baby," she said. KB pounded her walls until he reached his climax. She exploded first then KB gave her four hard, long, deep strokes before pulling out and busting on her butt.

*　　*　　*

Cliff couldn't believe he got caught slipping. He was knee deep in some pussy when he felt some hard steal smack against the back of his head. He knew that this bitch Tasha was a sneaky little bitch but the head and pussy was the bomb so he over looked some of the things she did. Now here he was in the back of the Motel tied up butt naked looking at Tasha's milk chocolate 5'10 frame. She was thick like peanut butter in all the right places with soft Faith Evans lips.

Cliff felt blood trickle down his neck from the gash on the back of his head. He dizzily watched as Tasha and her male associate tear up the hotel room. After another five minute search they found the money and the dope. "Here," the man said. "Take this to the car and wait while I take care of your friend." "Ahh Snooky," Tasha said shaking her head." You said you wouldn't kill him." "Just go to the fucking car. This shit is over you trifling bitch," Snooky said.

Snooky had a gut feeling that Tasha had feelings for Cliff because she wouldn't agree to set him up unless Snooky agreed not to kill him. He knew at that moment Tasha was getting soft because she never cared if the vic. died or not. "You promised me Snooky you wouldn't kill him," she said in an agitated tone. "Promises are meant to be broken," he said before turning his back to Tasha. She grabbed the bag with the dope and money in it and stormed out of the hotel room. Snooky pulled a thick plastic bag out of his pocket, a roll of duck tape, and a combat knife. "Well it's time to check out," Snooky said standing over Cliff. He placed the bag over his head and closed off all the holes with the tape. He then plunged the knife three deep times in his side under his left rib cage, piercing his lung. Blood splattered everywhere as Cliff's body shook violently. Snooky waited for three minutes before his body sat motionless in the chair.

Snooky made his way to his car but stopped because he had a feeling he was being watched. He hopped in the car and noticed Tasha wasn't there. He saw the black Nike bag, but no Tasha. He started to get out but felt cold steal pressed to the back of his head. "Nigga put yo hands on the steering wheel and if you move yo head gone be on the dash board," the gunman said as he patted Snooky down and removed his gun. "Man what's up?" Snooky asked nervously. "Shut yo bitch ass up, I don't wanna talk to you. Now crank the car up and follow that black van," the gunman said. Snooky started the car up and rode in silence as he thought about Tasha. He couldn't believe he let her catch him slipping like this. He fell for his own banana in the tail pipe and now it might cost him his life.

Snooky drove in complete silence as his kidnapper sat quietly in the back seat. Snooky contemplated jumping out that bitch on I-20 and making a run for it but the way cars were flying on the interstate, he decided against it. The van exited Houston School Road and made a left, passing a ranch. He followed the van down a narrow street that led to a small junk yard. The van pulled up in the junk yard and drove around to a small shack building and came to a stop. Two people hopped out the van that Snooky didn't recognize due to it being so dark. One of the dudes opened the slide door and grabbed somebody out the back. It was Snooky's girl, Tasha. They made eye contact then Snooky felt the cold steal press against his neck. "Get out and don't do nothing stupid," his kidnapper said in a calm cold voice. Snooky complied with the orders and climbed out. His kidnapper led him into a small office room in the shack building where he was reunited with Tasha. The two people other than Tasha that was in the room, Snooky noticed as Guillotine and Nephew. Once he saw them two he instantly knew who his kidnapper was and what this was all about. Once he was tied to a chair next to Tasha he soon accepted his fate.

KB emerged from a dark corner holding a black .357 Magnum in his hand. He stood over Snooky and stared him down before exchanging words. Tasha squirmed in her seat as tears constantly rolled down her cheeks. She knew that the kind of life her and Snooky was living, this was one of the outcomes of the games they played. She prayed silently for God to forgive her for all the dudes that she had set up that led to their deaths.

Tasha wasn't your typical hood rat. She was from a pretty good family and didn't have to witness the deep depths of poverty. She graduated high school and completed two years of college at Texas Southern University in Houston before being manipulated by her smooth talking boyfriend to help him set up local dope boys. After she successfully set up her first vic. by using her assets to whip him in, her boyfriend turned her on to a luxurious lifestyle. She eventually got addicted to the fast money and dropped out of college. When her boyfriend got locked up she moved back to Dallas and hooked up with Snooky to continue in the fast lane. Now here she was tied to a chair in the middle of a junk yard.

KB stared Tasha down and couldn't believe how such a beautiful girl could be involved with a bullshit ass nigga like Snooky. He wanted to spare her life but he didn't need her running to the police because he couldn't afford to go back to jail. He looked into her beautiful eyes, and then checked out her luscious body. He quickly erased all sympathy from his mind and got to the matter at hand. He knew that Tasha was a grimy bitch so she deserved what she had coming.

KB stood over Snooky as they locked eyes. KB smiled at the pitiful look on his face. "Well nigga I guess its check out time," KB said. "Man I didn't have shit to do with what happened to your homeboy," Snooky explained. "That's funny cause since the shit went down, you've been taking all the credit for the move," KB said. "Come on bro you know the streets will make some shit up just to see some action," Snooky said, trying his best to change KB's mind. "Well you should have took heed to what a nigga was sayin so accept the shit like a man cause it ain't no more life lines left," KB said raising the pistol and pointing it at Snooky's head. "Wait bro!" Snooky yelled. "Let my girl go she didn't have shit to do with this," he pleaded. "Nigga that's how the game go. My nigga Dough didn't have shit to do with it but his life wasn't spared." Snooky shook his head and turned toward Tasha, "I'm sorry baby. I love you," he said before KB pressed the Magnum against his skull, pulling the trigger and splattering blood and fragments everywhere. Tasha let out a scream and looked at Snooky. A patch of his head was missing from the impact exposing his skull. She closed her eyes as images of her life started flashing through her mind. [*Bak . . . Bak . . . Bak*] . . . Three loud shots of hot lead ripped through her body. Once her breathing stopped and her body went limp they disposed of the bodies.

*   *   *

CHAPTER 7

BJ was lying on his back as Lisa slowly bobbed up and down on his Johnson. She had truly improved on her head game since their last encounter.

"Mmmm . . . Damn shawty you doing a nigga right," BJ moaned as he enjoyed the tingling sensation running through his body. Lisa applied more spit to his shaft as she deep throated him and came up screw balling his piece. She licked the tip of his head while she jacked him off. "You like that?" she asked as she licked around his head. He leaned his head back and enjoyed the service. He felt himself about to explode but held his composure until he can get his pound game on. Lisa got off his head and kissed her way up to his neck as she climbed on top of him and slowly slid down his thick shaft. She moaned softly as his piece filled her warm honey hole. BJ didn't have the biggest dick but he was blessed with thick, 8 inches that he worked very well. Once she accepted all of him in her juice box, she placed her hands on his buff chest and threw her head back in pleasure, working her hips. She moved in a circular motion as BJ's dick worked her walls. "Ssss . . . mmm . . . Ohhh . . . yeah," Lisa moaned as she licked her lips and started to bounce on his dick. He sat up and Lisa wrapped her legs around his waist and continued to move her hips. BJ licked and sucked on her tittles and nipples until her nipples got hard. BJ softly bit down on one and applied pressure to the other one. "Mmmm . . . Sss . . ." Lisa moaned. "I like that baby," she said as her juices escaped from her pussy.

BJ laid her down missionary style and rubbed her swollen clit with two fingers as she rolled her hips in coordination with his fingers. He patted his dick head against her pussy lips, teasing her opening. "Come on daddy, don't tease me like that," she moaned. BJ inserted his thickness into her box and started with slow strokes. He licked and sucked on Lisa's neck, leaving a hicky. He picked up the pace and looked into Lisa's deep gray, exotic eyes. They both anticipated each other's orgasms as they filled the room with moans and groans. "Do that shit daddy . . . mmm . . . sss . . . I'm bout to fuckin explode," Lisa said as she lifted her hips up meeting his thrusts. BJ felt her shiver as he pounded her pussy like a gorilla beating his chest. He felt his dick blow up as he exploded inside of Lisa's pussy. "Aww . . . fuck," he said as he rested on her chest. Lisa's pussy muscles were still contracting from her orgasm and he could feel her womb closing around his dick. He kissed her full lips and rolled off of her, taking her in his arms and they cuddled. "Damn ma, you a fool wit it," BJ said smiling as he ran his fingers through her silky hair. "I've always enjoyed our time together," Lisa said as she rubbed his chest. BJ tried to keep his feelings mutual while dealing with Lisa because he was in love with Tara, but every time he dealt with Lisa he slowly began to feel for her. They laid back in each other's arms until they drifted off to sleep.

BJ was awakened by the ringing of his cell phone. He looked at the clock and it read 3:00 a.m. He cursed himself for slipping up and leaving Tara hanging. He promised her that they would chill at his spot tonight and make it a movie night. His intentions were to knock Lisa down and burn off, but after a night's long romp he found himself sleeping on his bonnie. BJ rolled from under Lisa and went into the kitchen to answer his cell. "Hello," he said clearing his throat. "Baby what's up?" Tara asked in a cool voice. "I thought we were going to chill tonight?" "I'm sorry ma. Some shit came up and I had to set something up for KB." "Damn you could have at least called. I've been at your spot since 10:00. Where you at?" she asked. "I'm in North Dallas with KB," he lied again. "You at my spot?" BJ asked. "Yeah," she answered. "Alright, I'm on my way," he said. Just as he hung up he felt a pair of hands touch him and he jumped back, startled. "Damn pimp chill out," Lisa said smiling. "Girl don't be doing that shit, creeping in the dark like that," he said wrapping his arms around Lisa's naked frame. "Who was that?" she asked softly, already knowing the answer. "Damn nosey," he said smiling. "You know who it was at 3:00 in the morning." She pulled out of his clutch, "mmmph," she sighed before walking off. BJ eye balled her naked frame walking away. She had every bit of 42 inches of ass that looked good with her shapely bo-legs. After he washed the sex off his body he made his way to the bedroom to get dressed. Lisa was laying in the bed with her back to him. "Ay shawty I'm gone get at you in a bit," he said. "Yeah whatever," she said in a dry monotone voice. "Turn yo ass around," BJ said firmly. Lisa knew he meant business and did as she was told. "Man I know you ain't copping affection on a nigga. What I tell you about all that?" He asked sitting on the edge of the bed. "I'm sorry. It wasn't nothing," she said submitting to his authority. They had been fucking around for about a month and Lisa wanted their relationship to be more than what it was but she knew BJ was in love with Tara. She had always loved BJ and since they reunited that old flame sparked. She liked everything about him including his swag, his looks, his touch, his smell, and his heart. From the streets to the sheets he was square business and he was also good with her daughter. Hell, she was a woman full of emotions and they were flowing right through her pores. This is exactly what BJ didn't want to happen. He let it be known before they started fucking that he had a main girl and wasn't leaving her, but he didn't want to straight dog Lisa out and make her feel like a piece of ass. That's why he would do shit for her and Lizzarah and now it was showing. "Look, don't start vexing on me Lisa," he said stroking her chin. "I got you," he assured her as he leaned in and lip locked with her. Lisa sucked it up and accepted what he had to offer for the moment. BJ made his exit and headed for his love nest where his Queen awaited.

*   *   *

Profit:

"Man chill the fuck down lil bro and tell me what happened," Profit said, giving his younger brother his full attention. "Man them niggas rode down on Snooky and his bitch, then left his body in a parking lot at Bruton Bizarre so people could see what he did," his brother explained as a tear dropped from his eye. "What made them niggas pull a stunt like that," Profit asked. His brother simply shrugged his shoulders but Profit read right through his bullshit. "Bren I need to know everything," Profit demanded. Bren explained everything from the incident at the party to him and creep riding down on KB, killing his homeboy. Bren felt bad that Snooky got done the way he did behind him being hot headed. Snooky was Bren and Profit's first cousin. Snooky and Bren were only a year apart and growing up they did everything together. Now he was just a memory. "Y'all niggas just in the streets renegading while I'm busting my ass trying to make shit easier," Profit yelled. "Now Snooky dead and I got some mo beef on my hands." "This is costing me a lot of cash lil bro, you need to calm the fuck down some and start using your fucking brain. You and mothafuckin Creep!" he said puffing on a black and mild.

Bren stood there as his brother's words went through one ear and out the other. He knew that his big brother was backed up by bread so his actions were covered. Him and Snooky didn't accept hand me downs so that's why they robbed whoever. They didn't want to live in Profit's shadow so they vowed to make a name for themselves by making niggas get down or lay down and now Bren is contemplating revenge.

*   *   *

A couple of months have passed and it was June of 2007. Club One was throwing a Juneteenth bash and everybody that was somebody would be there. The club owner had managed to get Lil Wayne, Bun-B, Plies, Rick Ross, DJ Khaled, and some local rappers to entertain the night. KB, BJ, and Nephew all pulled out their whips for the occasion. Guillotine, George, and Bam rode with KB. J-Note, Jeff, and Velt rode with BJ. LD and the tiwns, Malique and Tylique, rode with Nephew. Malique and Tylique were Nephew's younger brothers. At 19, Nephew had the two rock stars sitting lovely. Nephew took some of the money he made and invested into their rapping career. They dropped a mix tape and on occasions performed at some of the local clubs around Dallas. They got most of their fan base from rapping at parties that they usually promoted, plus their Myspace page was jumping. The trio pulled their whips up in the parking lot across from the club. They watched as people watched them crawl through the parking lot looking for somewhere to park. It was no doubt that people knew who they were and it showed as all eyes were on them. BJ stepped out of his car with smoke following. His trunk was basing to the sound of T.I.'s. hit single, "What you know about that." BJ was dressed to impress. He had on a red Red Sox baseball jersey. The jersey was all red with white lettering. He had on some all white Coogie leather shorts with red stitching. He had on the red and white Jordan 13's with a matching fitted hat. His neck was complimented by a 30 inch all iced out chain with a two deep-two real piece. On his wrist he rocked a 24K iced out Marc Jacobs watch. BJ felt good about his appearance and his status. It had been almost 2 years since his release and he was already ahead of most of his peers.

KB was rocking a very conservative lime green, Rockawear button down with the matching fitted hat.

He was rocking some Black Rockawear jeans with some lime green and white, low top, Air Force Ones. He wore a 46 inch, iced out doggy chain, iced out Marc Jacobs watch, with a lime green matching band and a pinky ring.

Nephew stepped out in an orange Polo Johnny Blaze shirt, some orange stitched replay jeans and some suede orange Filas. He had a Rose Gold 24K, 36 inch chain on with a Rose Gold diamond crushed watch and matching bracelet. The whole crew was flossed out looking like a million bucks and they wanted people to know they were rolling dough by the stacks. The line was long but they didn't have any intentions on standing in it. KB went straight to the bouncer and they exchanged greetings. KB pulled out a crispy one hundred dollar bill and they proceeded into the club. After they paid their $30, they mobbed through the crowd and laid eyes on some of the finest females Dallas had to offer. Everybody was in chill mode ready to get their drink on. They found a couple of tables in the corner close to the bar where KB could see the whole club and peep the scene. Nephew flagged a waitress down so she could make her way over to the two tables. "What can I help you fellas with?" she asked showing her pretty smile to compliment her pretty brown face. "Can we get four bottles of Hypnotic, three bottles of Grey Goose, and twelve long-neck Millers?" Nephew said smiling, showing the diamonds in his mouth.

The DJ was banging Flo-Rida's "Get Low." Every female in the crowd was bouncing asses and dropping it low. The waitress came back with another waitress to bring their drinks. Nephew pulled out a couple of c-notes and handed them to the waitresses. They all grabbed cups and began drinking. The crowd got hype when Lil Wayne, Plies, Rick Ross, and Bun B took the stage with DJ Khaled in the booth. They dropped song after song and got the club crunk. The crowd showed them a lot of love and in return the rappers made it rain as they threw small bills into the crowd. After they rapped a song that they were all on, they made their exit.

The usual DJ got back in the booth. "Yeah this how we get down at Club One, nothing but the best. The bar still open so let's keep this party jumping," he announces as he played a track from some local Dallas rappers called "Get It Big" by Trap Stars and everybody started doing the dance. BJ scanned the crowd and saw a familiar face. Once they made eye contact he waved her over. Her and her crew pushed their way through the crowd as they headed for BJ's table. He reached over and tapped Nephew on the shoulder. "Say bro, this that chic Lisa I was telling y'all bout," he said pointing as she made her way over and sat in BJ's lap, greeting him with a kiss on the lips. "Hey baby," she said. "What's up ma? You looking real good," he said smiling. "You like?" she asked as she turned in a circle to give him a full view. She was rocking a pink and white scarf skirt by H&M that showed off her full thighs. She was rocking some 3 inch, pink Steve Madden pumps to show off her perfect pedicure toes. Her hair was in micro braids and her skin was looking natural with some lip gloss to bring out the fullness of her lips. "Excuse me y'all, these are my home girls. This is Nona, Kitty, Jayla, and Yasmin," she said pointing to each home girl. Nina was a Latino beauty with long black, thick wavy hair with gold streaks. Her face reminded you of the likes of Eva Mendez. Her body was flawless. She was a firm 32D-24-41 and it was very rare that you find a Latino chic that fine. Kitty was a 5'5, baby-faced, yellabone beauty. Her hair hung just below her ears. She was nicely built with a 38C-25-39 frame. Jayla was the Amazon. She had smooth dark skin like Tara Hicks from Belly. She had hazel eyes which were slanted with some Gabrielle Union lips. She stood right at six feet even and she was thick in all the right places at 36DD-30-50; she definitely stood out the most. Yasmin was the shortest of the group at 5'0. She had a light brown complexion with hair that hung to her ass in one long Laura Croft, tomb raider ponytail. Her facial features were very exotic. She had aqua green slanted eyes, and some pretty thin lips. She looked a little like Laura London but her frame was more desirable. She was a perfect 34D-25-40. Her presence said sex appeal and she had a model walk that made the dough boys go crazy.

Once everybody got acquainted the mood was right. Malique and Tylique had scooped up the two fine brown skin honeys and were on the dance floor. KB and Jayla were chilling; talking and sipping. "So Jayla, where you from," KB said licking his lips. "I'm from Oakcliff," she answered. "Oh yea, what part?" "Singing Hills. Do you know a nigga named Money?" she asked, taking a sip of her drink. "What's his real name?" "Shameer." "Oh yeah, I know Money, he said smiling, showing his shinning grill. Him and Money were Muslim brothers. Money was also on the same unit as KB, Nephew, and BJ. He was still serving time. He had 18 years for a robbery and kidnapping charge. "That's my relative," she said. After a brief conversation, KB found out that Jayla worked as a beautician in Singing Hills Shopping Center. Jayla was 24, single, no kids, and bisexual.

On the dance floor BJ and the rest of the crew were enjoying themselves. Lisa was grinding all up on BJ's dick as he moved his hips in coordination with hers. They were dancing seductively as BJ's hands roamed and felt every inch of her frame. He slid his hand under her skirt and pulled her thong to the side so he could rub her soft moist pussy lips. "Mmm . . . damn shawty, you hot as hell," he whispered in her ear as he nibbled on it. She moved slowly with his finger as he found her opening. "Sss . . . mmm . . . that's what's up, right there daddy," she hissed. "What you doing when the club close?" BJ asked. "You daddy," she moaned. BJ pulled the juices from her wet pussy and licked his fingers. "That's a bet," he said as they locked lips and passionately kissed in the middle of the club. After a couple more songs BJ and the crew was throwing back long necks and getting crunk. Through the crowd BJ spotted someone he had been wanting to see out of place. He informed Nephew that he was about to confront him. Then him, Nephew, LD, and Tylique made their way over to his spot. BJ marched right into the dude's face and wasted no time pulling his card. "What's up Bowie nigga? I see you still hanging around," he said smiling, taking a swig from his long neck. "Man why you playing?" Bowie asked.

Bowie was with his crew JJ, Jamal, and Dre. With his boys behind him he didn't feel threatened by BJ's presence but still wanted to play it safe. "Nigga I'm gone give you a chance to re-nig on yo deal with the D.A. You got two months or its rest in peace," BJ said as he stepped up and whispered the words in Bowie's ear so only he could hear him. From somewhere deep down Bowie found the courage to push BJ out of his space. BJ flipped his long neck around and broke it across Bowie's head, then followed with a hard right, dropping him. That was the que for Nephew, Tylique, and LD to move on Bowie's crew. Before you knew, bottles and bodies were being thrown around. Malique, Jeff, J-Note, Bam, Velt, KB, George, and Guillotine joined the rest of their crew in a stomping marathon of Bowie and his crew. Before security could make his way to the scene KB rounded everyone up and they made their way to their cars. The night ended with other crews shooting at each other leaving two dead and three injured by the next morning.

*   *   *

CHAPTER 8

It was the middle of the summer and the dough had been rolling in for KB, BJ, and Nephew and when they got paid, the crew got paid so everyone was satisfied. It had been exactly two years since BJ touched down and he was content with his status. He had about $60 G's saved up, a condo, jewelry, clothes, two bad bitches, and a slab. BJ, KB, and Nephew graduated to scoring four bricks. Things were so good that every weekend they would take two bricks to Houston and let their homeboys, James and Chuck, get their hustle on. James was from the Southside of H-Town and Chuck was from the North from a well known hood called 44 Acres Holmes. Chuck really wasn't a dope boy. He was green to the game but his little brother was a thorough bread hustler so he held chuck down and made sure everything got sold. Shit was lovely.

KB, Nephew, and BJ were in KB's car riding down Camp Wisdom when BJ spotted Bowie going into Anita's Corner Store. "Hey swing up in this lot KB," BJ said pointing. "What's up nigga?" KB asked. "Nothing, fince to handle this nigga," BJ said smiling. "Dawg don't do nothing stupid," KB said seriously.

"I'm not, I just got to let this nigga know I'm for real," he said jumping out the car.

KB parked on the side of the store and they waited about five minutes until people hit the corner screaming. "HE GOT A GUN!" KB and Nephew jumped out, ran to the front and saw BJ beating this nigga down with his pistol. KB and Nephew pulled BJ off Bowie and drug him towards the car. "Your time running out bitch ass nigga," BJ yelled before they hopped in the care and burned off. "Man what's wrong with you?" KB yelled. "The nigga stole off on me. I wasn't gone pull out but the nigga was handling me bro." Nephew started laughing, "What you laughing at nigga?" BJ asked. "How you gone bring plex and end up getting handled?" he said. "Shit sometimes it happen like that, fuck you nigga."

KB pulled up in front of his spot on Kellog and saw two black Lexus' parked in front of his shit. All three of them recognized who the Lexus' belonged to so he parked his slab and they cocked their guns. Before KB got out of the car he called Guillotine. "Hello?" he answered. "What's going on?" KB asked. "Shit the nigga came in peace and said he needed to holla at you," Guillotine explained. "Alright, we're coming in."

They hopped out the car and went into the house with guns still in their hands. Profit was sitting in the living room accompanied by Flip, Booley, Barry, Bren, and Creep. They were standing around Profit like he was The Don. After a quick stare down, KB got to the situation at hand. "What's up?" KB said in a calm manner. "It's been a while huh?" Profit said lighting up a cigarette. "Nigga skip the small talk, we ain't homeys so speak yo peace," KB said sarcastically. "This nigga real ill," Bren said firmly. "We come in this bitch real respectfully and he still don't show no love. We should have came in blazing," Bren said before being cut off by Profit. "You wouldn't have done shit but signed yo papers for early release of yo life hoe nigga. Ain't no push overs over here," Nephew said holding his mug. "Look, check this out. One of my main spots got hit about a week ago, more bloodshed. I know how y'all get down. I'm gone chalk it as a lost. I'm here to get some kind of truce understood. This shit is costing me too much money and too much blood if you know what I mean," Profit said as he puffed on his Newport. "Eye for an eye, tooth for a tooth, life for a life. You knew about this game before you played, ain't no explanation needed. Stay out of our way and we stay out of yours. This ain't no one way thang," KB said reversing the role on Profit so he'll be the one making the call. KB read through his little plan the minute he started talking but it didn't work. "Well I guess that's a wrap then, huh?" "It was nice being in you fellas presence; let's roll my niggas," he said standing up, leading his pack rats out the door. He stepped in front of KB and stuck his hand out for a hand shake but KB stood his ground. Wasn't no deal or bet made so he saw no need to shake hands with a snake ass nigga like Profit. He knew Profit's plan was to try and catch them with their guards down.

*   *   *

"Man why you going through my phone Tara?" BJ asked furious. "All I did was answer it cause it kept ringing," she answered. "So you wait until a nigga hop in the shower to start snooping through a nigga shit," he barked. "Whatever nigga. Who is that freak bitch sending you them nasty text messages," she asked. "Man I'm trying to be as discrete as possible with what I do in the streets but with you crawling down a nigga back you making nothing outta something, Tara damn," BJ said as he dried his body. "No I ain't nigga. That bitch got you wide open don't she?" Tara said smiling as she stepped closer to BJ. "A bitch ain't good enough to have me wide open," he said as they locked eyes.

Tara really wasn't tripping about what he did in the streets. She too had friends the she would call every blue moon. It was understood between the two that they would respect each other's space and keep things drama free long as they kept their business out of each other's face.

Tara moved closer to BJ and started massaging his thick shaft. He moaned and passionately kissed her full brown lips, sucking the bottom one. "Why you be stunting on a nigga," he asked. "I just be fucking with you. I'm gone love you whether we are together or not. You my nigga," she said smiling as she pulled her tank top over her head exposing her perfectly shaped breasts.

All talking ceased as they fell into Dream's, Falsetto, playing on BJ's surround sound system. *"Falsetto . . . ooh . . . ooh . . . baby . . . ah . . . ah . . . baby."* They stood with their bodies locked as one while BJ slowly licked and sucked her perky chocolate nipples. He sucked on her titties like a new born baby. "You like that?" he asked as he applied enough pressure on her nipple to stimulate the rest of her body. Tara moaned in delight as BJ kissed down her body and fell to one knee. He pulled Tara's pretty purple thongs off and placed one of her long legs over his shoulder. She braced herself on the wall as she prepared to receive his tongue. "Mmm . . . sss . . ." she hissed as BJ rubbed his fingers across her swollen clit. He teased her slit before kissing her chocolate pussy lips. Tara was wet and ready to enjoy the pleasure. BJ licked up and down her slit and sucked on her lips as he played with her clit. "Aww . . . yes . . . that's it," she moaned placing her hands on his head. BJ licked around her hole before inserting his thick index finger. He worked her G-spot and clit as he slurped up her peach juice. "Aww . . . shit . . . I'm bout to cum daddy," she moaned as she worked her hips in rhythm with his finger. He finger banged her warm walls and diligently sucked her clit as her cum dripped from between her pussy lips with him licking every drop. Tara had to brace herself when she got light headed and knees were weak. BJ guided her over to the black lazy boy chair in the corner of the living room. She propped one leg on the arm and slightly bent the other one as she bent over ready to receive BJ's shaft. He rubbed her pussy lips with his dick head before entering her juice box. He started with slow deep strokes as he watched Tara's pretty chocolate pussy lips wrap around his thick dick. "Mmm . . . I like how you feel this pussy up," she moaned as she gripped the chair. Tara loved it when BJ hit it from the back; she could feel every inch of his dick as her tight walls wrapped around his piece.

"Damn shawty this shit good," BJ said as he started pounding her walls. The sound of balls slapping, wall clapping, and loud moans filled the room. Tara worked her pussy muscles as she came and came again. Her cum escaped from her pussy and was all on BJ's dick as he slowed up his pace. He pulled his dick out her pussy and her juices ran everywhere. BJ laid her on her back missionary style, placed both of her legs on his shoulder. "This what's up right here," he said. BJ slipped his super hard dick in her pussy and his tongue in her mouth. He rocked her walls as he felt them curving in. Tara arched her back and met BJ's thrusts as she closed her eyes and enjoyed the pleasure. BJ banged her pussy until she felt his piece get thicker. 'Aww . . . aww . . . pull out daddy," she moaned. BJ gave Tara five good hard, long pumps before pulling out and busting his warm nut on the front of her pussy. He rolled over exhausted, trying to catch his breath.

"Damn baby it's like that huh?" Tara said, smiling and satisfied with his performance. "I've been tense and stressed all week. Damn you got that fire lil mama," BJ said smiling. "Boy hush," she said playfully slapping his chest as she got up wobbly legged and went to take a shower. After they showered and made love under the water, they crawled in the bed and instantly fell asleep in each other's arms.

* * *

CHAPTER 9

Nephew and the twins pulled up in front of Lina's apartment and saw Lonzo's Lac parked out front. He thought about not going in but he knew he promised his son's granny that he would pick up her grandson and take him shopping. The twins stayed in the car while he went inside. Nephew made it to the door when heard muffled music coming from the apartment. He looked at his watch and realized it was too early for music to be banging that loud. It wasn't even 10:30 a.m. yet. He knocked on the door and waited for someone to come to the door. There was no answer. He knocked repeatedly, still no answer. He turned the knob and saw that the door was unlocked so he eased his way in the apartment. He could hear slow jams coming from the backroom. He checked the front room and saw that his son was sound asleep. Anger rose as he thought about how trifling Lina was. Now his intentions were to bust the party up. He was far from being a hater but he crept to the backroom anyway. As he got closer to the door he heard music and moaning. He turned the knob and busted up the party.

"Bitch what's up?" Nephew said enraged. Lina and Lonzo was startled by Nephew's grand entrance. Lina hurriedly jumped off of Lonzo and tried to cover up her naked body. "What's wrong with you? Don't be busting in my shit like this," she yelled as she threw on a shirt and some panties. Lonzo sat there for a moment, heated, as Lina pushed Nephew toward the living room. "Bitch don't touch me with yo dick beaters. You real fucking trifling," he said. "How the fuck you get in my apartment," she asked frowning. She felt embarrassed that her baby daddy caught her in the act of sexing her man. "Hoe the door was unlocked but fuck that." "You in there fucking that nigga in yo mama's bed with the door closed, music loud, and my son in there sleep by his damn self. Bitch I don't care what you and that nigga got going on but my son up in this bitch. You could have waited until I came and picked him up you disrespectful bitch," he yelled as he walked passed her to the room where his son lay. Down the hall Lonzo was standing in his jeans and wife beater t-shirt, watching the scene play out. He didn't care about Nephew or his son. "Whatever nigga, I do as I please. You don't pay no bills roun' here," she barked. Nephew wrapped his hands around Lina's neck, cutting of her air circulation. "Bitch don't play with me and don't be stupid," he said, pushing her out of his face. He gathered his son in his arms and walked out the room. He saw Lonzo standing at the bathroom door laughing. "What's so funny nigga?" Nephew asked. "You nigga," Lonzo barked with his smile turning into a frown. "Nigga don't buck in this while I have my son in my hands," Nephew ordered. "Fuck you and yo son nigga," Lonzo spat.

Nephew pulled out his cell phone and hit speed dial, calling Malique to come get his nephew. Malique and Tylique marched up the stairs, knowing something was about to go down. When they stepped in, Lina was in Nephew's face trying to get him to leave. "Just leave Marco. Please just go," Lina begged. Nephew handed his son to Malique and tried to march passed Lina. "No Nephew, get out." "Naw, I'm finna beat this hoe up," he said pushing Lina's small frame out of the way. Lonzo posted up and Nephew countered his stance. No words said they started duking it out.

"Whoop that hoe bro!" Tylique yelled, bouncing up and down laughing because Nephew was getting the best of Lonzo. "Stop. Stop. Malique stop them," Lina yelled. "Naw the nigga shouldn't have been bumping," Malique said smiling. Nephew caught Lonzo three times in the face opening a gash above his right eye. Lonzo staggered into the wall and Nephew rushed him and hit him two more times making his nose bleed. Lonzo grabbed Nephew and wrestled him to the ground. "Naw don't wrestle nigga," Nephew said. Lonzo was on top of him but before he could release the furry, the twins were on his ass unleashing a load of haymakers. Nephew managed to get from under Lonzo who was now balled up on the floor as the twins stomped him into submission. "Get off him," Lina yelled as she tried to grab Tylique.

"Alright y'all, let the nigga make it," Nephew ordered. Within seconds the twins stopped stomping him. Lonzo laid there groaning as blood dripped from his busted mouth and broke nose. Lina rushed to his aid and tried to help him up. He growled when she touched his side. "Look what y'all did," she said. "Next time he will think twice before he open his fucking mouth. Let's go twins," Nephew said. They gathered up his son and left Lina's apartment. Nephew didn't have no pitty for Lonzo. He deserved that ass whooping and he had plenty more to give. He knew with the kind of ass whooping he just gave Lonzo, he would retaliate but Nephew didn't trip cause he was ready to blaze.

*   *   *

It was a hot Sunday in August. KB, BJ, and Nephew had their cars parked side by side at Rochester Park. Rochester was a popular park in South Dallas where all the ballers and want to be ballers hung out on Sundays. There were different clicks that rolled together at the park. You have your too fast too furious car club, the motorcycle crew, the Chevy Caprice crew, the Cadillac crew, and the big body SUV crew. Then you had the small timers that would just roll through and add to the crowd. The females were plentiful; rocking everything from short shorts to too little short skirts. Their intentions were to make all the dope boys go crazy and hook as many ballers as possible. The shit was live.

BJ, Nephew, and KB were standing around the trunk of their slabs engaging in small talk. The twins, Guillotine, and J-Note were grouped up with some bitches. "Damn bro," BJ said, smiling and showing his diamonds. "Shawty fine than a bitch, I got to have that," he said making eye contact as her and her two home girls strutted by. BJ hopped off his trunk and stepped to the shorty. "Excuse me Miss Lady could I talk to you for a minute?" BJ asked, being polite as possible. She stopped and smiled, "I'm surprised you didn't just grab a bitch arm like the rest of these scavengers," showing her pretty whites. "Naw my mama taught me better than that and my sister taught me how to step to a female and get a good response. So how are you doing? I'm BJ," he said extending his hand. "My name is Kerri"

"Damn ma, you look just like Paula Patton," he said. "Who?" she asked, curious to know who he was comparing her to. "Have you ever seen the movie Déjà vu with Denzel Washington?" he asked. "Oh yea, you're talking about the lead actress," she said smiling. "She is pretty ain't she?" "Hell yeah, but anyways I know you trying to get your stroll on, so how bout you gone and drop ya boy your numba so we can chop it up later? Maybe in a more delicate atmosphere," he said smiling.

Once he got her number, her and her home girls walked away. BJ was content with his catch of the day. Kerri was a pretty, light brown beauty with short hair. She possessed a slender face, 38C cup breast, flat stomach, 25" waist, and a pretty round 40" apple bottom. She was about 5'4 and well toned. She had the shape of a volley ball star. He sat watched as her and her home girls strutted down the street and once she was out of sight, he hopped back on his trunk and smiled as he took a swig of his ice cold Bud Ice.

"Now that was a cute bad bitch. I bet she got some pretty toes, "he said smiling. "I gots to gal that one," BJ said as he contemplated adding another fly chick to his play list. Nephew and KB looked at each other and laughed, "Nigga don't start that shit! You can't gal every bitch you talk to," KB said laughing. BJ mumbled under his breath, "shit Benjamin say I can have whatever bitch come my way." "What that nigga say Nephew?" KB asked as he puffed on a blunt. "I don't know what his soft ass said; you know he got one of those fat lazy tongues," Nephew said laughing. "I said BEENNJAAMINN," BJ said slurring Benjamin on purpose.

Nephew and KB looked at BJ and asked "Who?" in unison. "These buffalo balls!" he said laughing and pointing at both of them. "Aww . . . . you got down, but BLAAACK gone beat that ass if you slip," Nephew said slurring the word black." "Who?" BJ asked. KB jumped off his trunk and grabbed his crotch, "that's who, right here hoe ass nigga," KB said laughing. Nephew joined and BJ smiled as he drunk the rest of his Bud. "Man I can't win with you two niggas so fuck it, eatmadick," he said real fast. "What!" Nephew asked. BJ smiled and pointed at his piece. "Here this nigga go with that RuPaul shit. Soon as a nigga start deez nuts jokes, this nigga get on some punk shit," Nephew said smiling. "Fuck you nigga you stay on dem," BJ said. "On what?" replied Nephew. KB jumped off the hood and grabbed his crotch again, "dem nuts hoe ass nigga," BJ said laughing hard. KB and Nephew joined in.

It was times like these that they all enjoyed. It was nothing like getting money, fucking bitches, and having fun. They all appreciated each other's loyalty towards one another and it showed in a major way; nothing like having some real ass niggas by your side. KB, Nephew, and BJ trusted each other and together they vowed to come up and treat each other like brothers. That part wasn't hard because KB and Nephew were blood related but it was times when BJ would feel left out but every time KB would assure him that they were locked in and he would be down for him no matter what.

The twins drove Nephew car down M.L.K. and J-Note led the pack as he drove BJ's car. Nephew, BJ, Guillotine, and KB were all in his car as they rode the streets. M.L.K. was the spot everybody would hit after they left Rochester Park. It reminded you of Crenshaw in L.A.; females, cars, ballers, even the non-ballers hanging out. They parked their cars on the curb and chilled. "This what's up," KB said as he puffed on a hydro-filled gar. "These niggas be in this spot deep slipping, cash and dope everywhere. Jayla gave me the run down," KB said.

"Do you trust that hoe?" Guillotine asked as he took a sip from his syrup filled cup. "Yeah, I done slang cock to this bitch and she gave me her whole life story. I checked these niggas out and they real soft. They done got too comfortable in they hood. Guess they feel like won't nobody try em," KB said passing the blunt to BJ. "Where they at?" BJ asked inhaling a load of smoke. "In Singing Hills," KB answered. "Well shit, let's do it then," Guillotine said."

"Y'all niggas got some throw aways?" KB asked, reaching for the blunt BJ was babysitting. They all shook their heads yeah. "Well this the jump," When we leave here, I got this dope fiend rental. I'm going in to try to score an ounce and hopefully I get the jump on them niggas once I dr . . . ." KB was interrupted by a concerned BJ, "Hold up, let me get this straight. You going in with no mask?" he asked. KB shook his head yeah. "Then we must finna commit to felony ones then?" BJ asked. "What's the problem?" KB asked. "No problem, just wanted to get everything understood," he said sitting back.

His thoughts took him back TDC, waking up early in the morning to go to work in the fields, lock downs, and being told what to do 24/7. That shit didn't sit right with BJ but he was already committed to do whatever to reach the top so the thought of money cleared his mind and he snapped out of trance.

KB went over the plan explaining the set up again and once everybody was on the same page that was a wrap, it was going down. At about 11:45 that night they pulled to the spot in a black 4-door, 2001 Pontiac Grand AM. KB checked on everybody one last time before getting out the car. He made it to the door and knocked. After about 45 seconds he was let into the spot. Guillotine, Nephew, and BJ all waited anxiously and silently in the car. BJ looked at Guillotine who was always nervous when it came to licks like this. He really wasn't down for running in traps and shit cause only three things could happen; a lucky get away, death, or jail. But the wheels were in motion so it was too late for anyone to back out.

[Sounds of sniffing . . .], "man which of you nasty ass niggas pooted?" Nephew asked, looking at Guillotine. "Man why you look at me nigga? I can hold my mud," Guillotine said. Nephew looked at BJ who was looking out the window. "BJ bitch!" Nephew said. "Nigga just a lil nervous, just chill though I don't smell shit." Nephew rolled his window down. "I know I ain't the only nervous mothafuka in this bitch." BJ said looking at both of them. They didn't say nothing, just started smiling. "You can stay in the car if you want to, be the get away driver," Nephew said sarcastically. "I said I was nervous not sced hoe nigga." Guillotine's phone started going off. He looked at the ID and saw it was

KB. "That's our que right there, let's go," Guillotine said. They all jumped out the car and BJ put on a black ski mask. Nephew and Guillotine stopped and looked at him. "Why you got a mask on?" Nephew asked. "Just being cautious," BJ replied. "Nigga ain't gone be no witness left," Nephew assured him.

"Nigga stop worrying bout me, let's go," BJ barked. They walked up to the door and went straight in KB had both dudes inside held down at gun point. KB looked up as his goons walked through the door. He smiled when he saw BJ was the only nigga with a mask on. "Bro why you got on that hot ass mask?" "Being cautious," he said real fast. Guillotine went straight to the kitchen with the back pack and tore it up. KB continued to hold the two trappers down as BJ and Nephew went to search the two backrooms. Nephew stopped at the first one and went to work. The back room door was cracked so BJ pushed it open. As he stepped in he was met with a hot slug to the shoulder. The force made him stagger back into the hallway. The gunman fired two more slugs at BJ before he was able to take cover in the bathroom. Nephew peeped around the corner as the gunman shot six more times before the clip went empty, *[click . . . click . . . click].*

Nephew heard the click and rushed the gunman, as he ran toward the bed where a shotgun was laying. Nephew unloaded four shots catching the gunman in the back with each one. The gunman laid motionless on the floor as Nephew pumped two more in his body. Guillotine ran down the hall with his gun aimed ready to let loose. "Nephew!" he yelled. "I'm cool," Nephew yelled back. "I ain't though," BJ yelled from the bathroom. Nephew and Guillotine went in the bathroom and saw BJ laying in the tub holding his shoulder. "Man that bitch shot me twice bro!"

"Dawg how you let a female bang on you like that?" Guillotine asked, smiling. "Man y'all stop playing and get me to a hospital." They all jumped when they heard five shots ring out loud. KB yelled from the front, "Man what you niggas doing? Let's go," he said. Nephew ran to the back room and ram shacked it. In less than two minutes he found two birds and stacks of money in plastic bags. Nephew and Guillotine helped BJ to the car while KB cleaned up BJ's blood with over a gallon of bleach. He ran to the car, jumped in and they headed to Parkland Hospital, listening to BJ whine about how far that was and that he would be dead by the time they got there. By the time they reached the hospital he had blacked out.

*   *   *

CHAPTER 10

BJ had suffered an in and out shoulder wound, as well as an in an out buttocks wound. They kept him two days to run tests on him before he was released.

KB went to his spot and dropped off ten G's and a half of brick and BJ gave him the business. "Nigga I almost got smoked for 10 G's?" he asked as he limped to the kitchen and poured himself a shot of Grey Goose. "Damn bro, the niggas ain't have shit but 50 G's, about 10 pounds of dro and two birds," KB explained as he sparked up a fat ass blunt of Dro. "What's that?" BJ asked looking at the fat blunt. KB hit it hard then bounced his shoulders up and down as he exhaled the smoke and smiled, "this that bank head right here." "Where mine at? BJ asked, reaching for the blunt. KB lifted up his shirt and pulled out two compressed Ziploc bags filled with Hydro. "Here you go bro," he said handing BJ the bags and reaching for his blunt. "What you gone do with that shit?" KB asked. BJ smiled and did the shoulder lean with his good shoulder. "I'm finna smoke all that. Fuck the world. I'm finna lay up for about two weeks and get high all day and night," he said dapping KB up. "I feel that. Hey you know that bitch that was in the trap?" KB asked. "Yeah what's up." Man she wasn't nothing but 18, just graduated from S.O.C." KB said shaking his head. "Well that bitch banged that iron like she was 30. If she would have swung that bitch and held it right I would probably be dead so fuck her. Wrong place, wrong time," BJ said as he sat down on his leather sofa, leaning on the good ass cheek. KB shrugged his shoulders, "Well anyway me, Nephew, and the twins going to H-Town this weekend to take some shit to Chuck and James. You rollin?" KB asked. "Fuck H-Town! Naw I'm chillin. This is a perfect time for me to spend some time with Tara. But tell James and Chuck I said boom on that shit," he said smiling. BJ and James would always city trip with each other but in the end it was all love. "We'll probably stay the whole weekend," KB said. "Yeahhh, I know what's up?" BJ said, pointing his finger at KB. "What nigga?" KB said. "You and Ne finna do a lot of pillow talking and heavy breathing," he said. "Stay out my bidness nigga, but shit you know what's up. Shawty fine as fuck and she got that good," KB said, dapping BJ up. "Gone and burn off bro and tell Nephew to come wash a nigga draws or something," he said laughing. KB walked to the door and stopped, "Oh yea, you didn't call that nigga?" KB asked. "Who?" BJ replied. KB grabbed his crotch and said, "Dick Tracy nigga," and ran out the door.

* * *

Jeff and Bam were at KB's spot on Kellogg holding it down while KB and Guillotine were in Houston. Jeff was bagging up some ounces when he heard a loud knock on the door. *[BAM . . . BAM . . . BAM . . . BAM . . . BAM]*, he jumped because the knocks startled him. His first thought was the police but they had some lookouts to warn them of a sting or raid and they had police scanners to stay up on things. But being in the game you could never be too careful.

"Man what the fuck!" Bam yelled coming out the back room *[BAM . . . BAM . . . BAM . . . BAM]* "Nigga shhhh," Jeff said. "Here take these in the bathroom just in case. If I yell police, flush them hoes," Jeff said, holding about nine ounces. *[BAM . . . BAM . . . BAM]*. Bam ran to the bathroom in the backroom and locked both doors. Jeff eased to the door and checked the peep hole. It was dark so all he could make out were two black jackets with white lettering that read, D.P.D. He cracked the door and peeped out. Once he got the door cracked it was bomb rushed and knocked off the hinges. The gunman entered the house and before Jeff could make a move they filled him up with bullet holes leaving him in a bloody mess in the middle of the floor. The head gunman started backing orders, "Hey you hit the backroom, you hit the front and I got this up here. Let's make this fast," he said.

Bam heard the shots and knew it wasn't the laws. He dropped the ounces by the toilet and pulled his two all black 9 Berettas off his hip. He peeped his head out the bathroom in time to see one of the gunmen flipping the mattresses. He took a deep breath and held his guns up as he rushed out the bathroom. The gunman was caught off guard as Bam filled his body with about five bullets. He cut the lights off and hid beside the flip up mat looking through a standup mirror so he could see down the hall. When the others heard the gunshots they came to the door and squatted by the entrance. "Shhh . . . go through that bathroom door so we can corner him in," the head gunman ordered. Bam saw one of the gunmen go through one of the rooms that connected to the bathroom he just came out of. It led to the room where he was hiding in. Bam had a clear shot at the door way so he stuck his left hand through the rails and when the gunman appeared in his view he let off seven shots, catching the gunman with three; two to the torso and one through the neck. The head gunman peered around the corner and Bam let off the rest of the shots in one of his Berettas. "Yea nigga! I'm on some Max Payne shit, you better spare yo life nigga," Bam said pulling a Glock .45 Taurus with a beam from behind his back. The gunman swung a Tech 9 in the room and let of some desperate rounds, *[tat . . . tat . . . tat . . . tat . . . tat . . . tat . . . tat]*.

Bam pointed the beam at the mirror and it reflected off the mirror targeting the gunman's chest. "Look at that nigga, you dead, this yo last time to spare yo life," Bam yelled. Bam knew he couldn't hit him from where he was but he had to think quickly. The gunman heard sirens in the distance and made a run for the exit. He sprinted down the hall and out the door, disappearing in the night. Bam got up from his spot, went in the restroom and flushed the dope down the toilet. Within minutes police had the spot flooded. Bam told them what happened and due to law procedures, they had to treat it as a robbery/ homicide until further investigation.

*   *   *

BJ had been hanging around the crib bored. Tara had to go to Atlanta to check out West Georgia College so she would be gone for a whole week. He had spent two days sexing Lisa the best he could with a fucked up shoulder and bum leg. He was sitting on the couch smoking a blunt just thinking about the last year he had been out. Things were lovely besides all the beef that was going on. He really wanted his nigga Dam-Dam out with him but shit wasn't looking too good for him. BJ told him to get something he could do and cop a plea and if he had to do some time BJ would hold him down. BJ knew the system all too well and even though they had a weak case, he knew that in trial them fucking crackers would still find him guilty and throw away the key. He thought back to the day he was sitting in front of an all white jury, all white D.A., and an all white judge, holding shit down. He thought about his family sitting behind him and his black scary ass, paid for lawyer sitting next to him. Once shit hit the fan he knew he was doomed. They made him into a killer even though he had never killed anyone. They made him into a big time drug lord and at that point he had only seen two keys in his whole life. They made him out to be a robber, a monster, and every other stereotypical characteristic they can put on a black man in the white man's judicial system. He sat there nervous as the jury read the verdict on his possession of 2.8 grams of crack and pistol case. "Guilty! Guilty!" After only ten minutes of deliberation them crackers found him guilty and the judge gave him 25 years in T.D.C.J. then retired; sorry son of a bitch. He could still hear the judge's last words replaying in his head, "I am going to make an example outta you."

BJ sat on the couch and smoked himself into a daze. He wanted to talk to somebody bad, Kerri. It had been a week since he got her number. He flipped his phone open and dialed her number. "Hello," she answered in the sexiest voice ever heard by a man. "May I speak to Kerri?" he asked. "This is she." "Hey this BJ, how you doing?" "Oh so you finally decided to call?" He smiled, "I didn't want you to think a nigga was a bug-a-boo." "Boy stop," she said chuckling. "Naw on the cool, it's been a busy week but shit I got some chill time on my hands so what's up?" he asked puffing on his sweet. "Nothing just got back from Denton."

"What you got going on that way?" he asked. "Damn somebody nosey," she said laughing. "Naw I had to go pay the deposit for my classes." "Oh so you a school girl huh?" "Yeah gots to get that edu-ma-cation." "If you don't mind me asking, how old are you?" "I'm 21, starting my Junior year at U.N.T., no kids, and I'm single. I am studying theatre arts and designing; oh and business," she said smiling on the other end. "Now that's what the fuck I'm talking bout! A sista that's bout her business." She laughed, "boy you crazy."

"So you don't play no sports?" "Yeah volleyball," she replied. "Now it's my turn. Fill me in on some of your business." "I'm 24, in an open relationship, no kids, own apartment, own car, own money, self-made businessman, oh and a romantic Pisces," he said exhaling and coughing. "What you doing boy?" "Mmmph now you being nosey," he laughed. "I'm smoking a blunt, want to hit it?" he asked, holding the blunt to the phone. "Don't smoke," she said firmly.

"Stop lying, I know you ain't miss goody." "I like to drink a lil bit but I don't smoke weed or do ex."

"Where you from?" BJ asked. "North Dallas, and you?" "Kiest-n-Polk," he said proudly. "Oh so you a B-Dawg huh?" "I represent but I don't do no tripping, I'm banging this money. Anyways when we gone hook up?" he asked. "Whenever you want to, yo girl won't trip will she?" Kerri asked sarcastically. "Let's get some things understood shawty. We both grown, we both trust each other. I said we have an open relationship so we do as we please and if it's meant to be then I'm gone lock her down," BJ explained. "I didn't mean to invade," she said. "I was gone let you know what the business was anyway. I'm not into games and secrets and shit. I want shit to be in the open so won't nobody feelings get hurt," he said with confidence. "So basically you want to play in my goods?" she said giggling. "Naw I want to get to know you. Don't get me wrong, your body and cute face is what got my attention but I wanna know if you got that same beauty on the inside, and if we happen to feel the chemistry and we end up fucking, I'm not gone turn it down. We grown, we should be able to handle shit like that," he said taking another puff from his sweet. After about another hour of talking to Kerri, BJ made him something to eat, popped a handle bar and fell asleep, pain free.

*   *   *

It had been a couple of days since KB's spot got licked. Bam was in the county in the north tower on the sixth floor. He was charged with two third degree murders and his bond was set at $250,000. For the last two days he had been watching the news and his story was main stream. He couldn't get in contact with anybody. The two dudes killed wasn't familiar to him; 22 year old Corey Butler and 20 year old Marvin Marshall. At first his mind was on Profit but once he saw the pictures and names of the two deceased, things were a blur. He figured it was a random pick. Over the two nights in the county all he could see was his homeboy, Jeff, stretched out with his body full of slugs. A couple of dudes in his tank would try to talk to him but he wasn't really the social type.

"Chow time, chow time," the officer at the door yelled. Bam hadn't ate in two days and his stomach was touching his back. He jumped off his bunk, slid on his orange shoes, and walked down stairs. Once he got to the front of the line he recognized the officer. "L.T. what's up nigga?" Bam said smiling. "Damn nigga, what up?" L.T. replied. "It's been a while," he said.

L.T. knew Bam, Jeff, J-Note, BJ, George, and Velt very well. They all attended the same high school at one point. When they were sophomores, L.T. was a senior. Him, Jeff, and J-Note were classmates.

"Yeah, a nigga been getting at this money huh?" Bam said. "Nigga I seen you all the news, you straight?" L.T. asked. "Not really bro, I can't get in touch with nobody. You know these phones don't call out to no cell phones and either everybody out of town or laid up."

"Well when I finish feeding, I am gone pull you through that side door into the gym and let you make some quick calls," L.T. assured him before walking off.

Bam demolished the three trays L.T. gave him and after they did 8:30 count, L.T. did what he said and pulled him out. He dialed BJ's number first. "Hello," BJ answered. "Nigga this Bam I need yo help," he said. "Where you at dawg?" BJ asked. "I'm in the county. You ain't heard what happened?" Bam asked. "Naw nigga, you know I've been out of commission."

"Well Friday night some niggas tried to hit KB spot. Me and Jeff were there. They killed Jeff and I downed two of them fools but the other nigga got away. My bond $250,000," he explained.

"Alright, I'm on my way, who cell you on," BJ asked. "L.T. fucked with ya boy," he said. "Oh yeah! Tell him I said what's up."

After BJ got off the phone he sat there in a daze and thought about what Bam had just told him. His mind was stuck on the fact that Jeff was dead. Fuck. Did J-Note know? He got up and limped to his room; pulled $25 G's from his safe, put on some clothes and headed for David's Bail Bond. On the way over he called J-Note and told him everything. As expected, J-Note went in a rage. That was J-Note's first cousin, they were close like brothers.

BJ went and picked Lisa up from Cedar Hill and by 10:45pm they made it to David's Bail Bond. After an hour of filling out paper and dropping 25 stacks, BJ and Lisa headed downtown to Lew Sterrit County Jail to wait for Bam's release.

*　　*　　*

It had been a month since KB's spot got hit and Jeff was killed. Summer was over and everybody was in full fledge hustle mode. KB took a $30,000 lost. Velt and George got jammed up with $15,000 cash and half a brick. So in all including bond and lawyer fees, they took about a $45,000 lost together. BJ was trying to get his $25,000 out the streets. J-Note was tearing up the streets trying to find out who killed his cousin so he put about $10,000 in the streets for info on anybody that was capable of pulling such a stunt. Nephew, LB, and Marcus took a $15,000 lost in North Dallas. Their spot got raided but they managed to get away.

Profit and his team was just that. All Profit. With all them grinding, stacking, and keeping a low profile; they managed to scrape up $100,000 in the mean streets of Dallas. Profit was now able to step his Kilo game up to par and cop 20 for 5 G's apiece and putting his money back in the streets to triple.

KB had been kicking it strong with Pedro Mercardo, Diaz's nephew. With Pedro fucking with him, KB swallowed his pride and him and his team was able to get 5 birds on front for 12.5 apiece. Pedro handled his Uncle's street business and found many prospects in the city to move as many birds as possible. Pedro took a liking to KB and his crew after he saw how street savvy they were. Even though they were taking lost after lost, they never laid it down and he liked their determination.

BJ and Kerri were kicking it strong. He wined and dined her to the fullest and even took her shopping. BJ liked Kerri's humbleness, her playfulness, and the chemistry was forming between the two of them. When they were together they acted like high school kids and BJ cherished every moment of it. Due to his savage ways and determination to hustle, he missed a lot of fun high school moments. Kerri liked BJ's company. When they were together he would transform from a hustler to Casanova and he kept a smile on her face. She was delighted that he had never made any sexual advances towards her in the months they were involved. Yeah he flirted and said freaky stuff on the slide but he was never pressed about getting her goods and she liked the respect he had for her.

*   *   *

CHAPTER 11

KB and his main girl, Stacy, been spending some much needed quality time together. Stacy put KB on pussy restriction after she found Jayla's number in his dresser. KB wasn't really tripping because he knew Stacy wasn't going anywhere. For the past three days, KB shut everybody out and ducked off to get his thoughts together so he can deal with his frustrations and stress caused by the streets. When he finally came back on the scene of course he had to hear Nephew and BJ's mouth about his disappearing act. Once he laced them up on the business they let it go. Stacy was a different story.

"Hell naw nigga!, where the fuck you been?" Stacy jumped up and yelled as soon as KB walked through the door. "Damn man chill out. I've been trying to get my mind right," KB said pulling his shirt over his head, exposing his coiled chest and tight six pack. "Nigga I ain't dumb. You prolly been laying up with that bitch," she said pushing KB's head with her index finger. "Look, shut up and don't touch me no more. How bout you calm the fuck down," he said calmly. "I ain't been with no damn body. If you would have checked you woulda known I was at my mama's house collecting my thoughts, damn just enjoying some me time," he said as he walked passed Stacy, stripping out of his clothes heading to the shower.

Stacy stood there with her arms folded as she heard KB crank the shower up. "No he didn't just shush me," she said to herself. She marched to the bathroom and banged on the door, "Nigga you got me fucked up! You don't hug or kiss me, you just come hop in the shower after three days. You must be trying to hide something." "I ain't got shit to hide! Now get yo ass away from the door," he yelled as he rested under the shower head. "Fuck you KB," she said as she marched back in the living room. KB hopped out the shower butt naked with water dripping off his body and stormed out the bathroom in pursuit of Stacy. She was standing in the middle of the living room wide eyed as she watched KB's snake swing left to right. He stepped in her space, "Look got dammit I don't have shit to hide, I'm a grown ass man so chill the fuck out," he said raising his voice.

KB could tell she was in heat. He grabbed the back of her neck as they shared the most exotic, aggressive kiss a couple could share. Stacy held her breath as KB sucked her warm tongue. Her pussy instantly caught fire and KB could feel the heat rise from between her legs. He aggressively ripped off her tank top exposing her nice firm breasts and did the same with her booty shorts. Stacy's pussy started dripping when KB man handled her boy shorts, exposing her bald shaved caramel pussy. KB examined her body before devouring her breast, sucking and squeezing each nipple until they stuck out like deer horns. He gave her little tender kisses checking her sexual barometer and it was off the charts. Stacy's built up tension and the energy she possessed transferred to KB as his every touch stimulated her body. KB had her butt naked in the living room touching her skin as she shivered with ecstasy. Nipples hard, intense kisses, KB knew he had her aroused. With his hand between her legs her infinite wetness soaked his fingers; she was ready. KB took his index and middle fingers and rubbed up and down her moist slit as his thumb massaged her swollen clitoris. Stacy arched her back as pleasure took over her body. She moaned softly as he played in her juice box, "ssssss . . . . ahhhhh . . . . this feels so good," she whispered as she rotated her hips in motion with his fingers. He dipped his head between her legs and licked the honey that was flowing from her pussy. KB slowly ran his tongue between her pretty thick pussy lips as he took her fold in his mouth and gently sucked on them like a Georgia Peach. "Ahhh . . . shiitt . . . . ssss," she hissed as her eyes rolled to the back of her head. She could feel the tingling sensation all through her body. KB sucked on her clit like a cherry push pop as his middle finger worker her G-spot. He licked and sucked, sucked and licked as juices gushed from between her lips. Stacy tried to squirm away but KB gripped her ass and moved his thick tongue in and out of her pretty pink hole. "Ssss . . . this pussy . . . . bout . . . . to . . . explode," she moaned, tensing up ready to release her sweetness. "Gone and cum for me baby," KB said as he flickered his tongue back and forth, up and down, round and round over her clitoris while he finger banged her to new heights. She shivered, cursed, moaned, groaned, and cursed some more as her cum squirted out of her hole. KB continued to finger please her as he watched her pussy spit up. "Awww . . . . shiiit . . . . fuck yeah!" she yelled, taken by her own orgasm.

KB flipped her over on her stomach and she immediately arched her ass up, offering him ecstasy with no hesitation. He spread her butt cheeks and found fondled with her pink before he entered her. Stacy closed her eyes tight and leaned her head back as she patiently waited to be fucked. He put his long, thick shaft against her warm wet wound and moved it up and down with his dick head. He stimulated her clit with the head of his dick as he watched her anticipate his next move. She moaned as he slowly entered her hot, fleshy folds. So nice, he thought to himself. Slowly, he spread her tight walls a little at a time as he worked about seven good inches in and out of her. Her juices popped and dripped, "Yes . . . give me . . . that dick," she moaned in between pumps. With her mouth open, KB leaned forward with slow strokes and licked her full lips. He sucked her tongue as he felt her body change and her tight walls wrap around his bulging dick. He could hear her breathing go from smooth to choppy. As KB stroked her thoroughly, he let out a husky growl and low moans to let her know that the pussy was good. "Fuck me nigga," she barked as she chunked that size 40 ass at him. He braced himself and forced the whole nine into her tight pussy touching the roof. She jumped, he gripped her ass cheeks as he rammed into her flesh like a savage giving her nothing but long deep strokes. She cursed and came, "aww . . . fuck you killing this pussy," she yelled as she buried her head in the carpet feeling his dick in her stomach. KB felt his climax rising as he pounded her pussy. He sped up and she moaned, cursed, and cried from pleasurable pain. He gave her five long hard strokes before pulling out shooting his hot nut on her back and ass. Out of breath, he rolled over on his back and stared at the ceiling in a daze. Stacy rolled on her side and rubbed her throbbing, aching, dripping pussy. She rubbed her stomach, got up and ran to the restroom to empty her bladder.

*   *   *

It was the middle of October and KB and his crew had managed to stack a grip and up their car game. BJ bought a candy red four door BMW MS Series, with cocaine white seats, red tint, and some 20 inch red and chrome Zen rims, made by Hypnotic Wheels. He put four 10's in the trunk and had four T.V. screens, two in the head rests. He had a laptop installed in the roof and one coming from the CD player. Lovely!

Nephew managed to cop him a cocaine white, 2006 Escalade Hybrid. He put Limo tint on all of the windows and all white seats. He had some 28" dub spinners. KB was rolling a 2006 money green Lexus GS400. The insides were money green with white stitching; Four T.V's and two 15's on deck producing a crisp thump. He had his ride sitting on some 20" chrome Ganja floaters, customized by DUB. They all contemplated butterfly and suicide doors but knew it would be too extreme.

They were back at that level to where they could get birds from Diaz at a good price, no front. After licking a couple of dope boys, things were looking good for KB, BJ, Nephew, and their protégés. Lately BJ had been spending time with Lisa, Kerri, and Tara. Shit was getting thick for him because Lisa was falling in love, Tara was demanding more of his time, and Kerri was getting soft hearted behind him. He wined and dined Kerri whenever she was in town and not only that, she was impressed with his dick game.

Nephew was still having baby mama drama with Lina. One day him, the twins, and LD were at the club chilling with Yazmin, Kitty, and Nina when Lina and some of her low budget hood rat home girls came strolling through the door. Once they spotted each other he knew it was going to be trouble. Nephew ducked off in the back of the club with Kitty and it wasn't long before Lina spotted them all hugged up. She strolled her conniving ass over there and dry picked an argument with Nephew. Lina started disrespecting Kitty with the name calling of bitches and hoes. That's when all hell broke loose. Kitty ended up beating the shit out of Lina and Lina's home girl Tay tried to jump in, followed by another of her flunkies. Nephew broke an empty bottle over Tay's head and shit got wild.

*   *   *

"Say bros this what's up," KB said as him, BJ, and Nephew were rolling through X-Line to drop some work off. "Pedro gone put me down with 50 pounds of Dro and 1,000 X pills. He want 45 G's for the Dro and 5 G's for the pills. What y'all bark lookin like?" he asked. "Man bro I got about 10 G's on me right now and a little over 70 G's in my stash," BJ explained as he puffed on a sweet. "Nigga why you got so much cash on you?" KB asked, looking through the rearview mirror. "Bro I ain't never had this much cash. I'm just stuntin like my daddy right now," BJ said smiling. "Alright bro! Somebody gone stunt and lick yo ass out here with all that dough in yo pocket," KB said turning into his homeboy's driveway. "Dang just chill. I'm gone be cool," BJ replied. "Anyways, Nephew what you holding?" "I got about 5 G's on me and about 90 G's in the stash," he said as smiled showing off his diamonds. "Damn man! Nigga in less than five years we damn near some six-figure niggas. Shit if we count the money we done lost, spent, and tricked off shit we'll probably be close to three quarters of a mill," KB said. "Yeah and you know we gotta keep niggas straight so shit I'm content. I'll probably go Hollywood if I got too much money," BJ said smiling. "We need to open up an afterhours or something," KB suggested. "But in due time we'll talk bout that," he said getting out the car.

After KB made the drop and picked up his cash, they headed to Town East Mall and sis some shopping. Life was good . . . . for now . . . .

*   *   *

CHAPTER 12

They all agreed to drop 17 G's apiece and cop the 50 pounds and thousand X-pills. BJ was too reluctant about coming out of his pocket so him and J-Note had a lick set up on this jarhead named Herb. He had a syrup and powder house in Oak Cliff in a hood named Wood Town, off Camp Wisdom and Polk. BJ felt safe with running in this spot with J-Note cause he didn't have a problem letting his guns blaze. J-Note didn't have no sympathy for nobody ever since his cousin got gunned down so his mentality was; if you wasn't close friends or family then nothing else mattered. It was cut throat.

They pulled up in front of Herb's spot in a stolen Mustang. "Alright, this what's up. I'm going in with this choppa blazin everything, can you handle that pistol grip sawed off Mossberg?" J-Note asked. "Nigga do a cat meow? Do a Kangaroo hop? Hell yeah I can handle this heavy metal," BJ said smiling, admiring the black chrome gauge action. "You got yo vest on tight and right?" J-Note asked. "Like a mothafukin jimmy hat," BJ said pumping the Mossberg.

"Well let's do this move fast bro. Safe in the front room floor, no code, just a key. It should be a tall nigga in here with braids, that's Herb and he has the key," J-Note explained.

BJ sat in silence thinking about TDCJ and about the lick they hit in Singing Hills when that young bitch shot him up. He took deep breaths and erased his negative thoughts.

(Sniff . . . Sniff . . .) J-Note twisted his nose up, "damn bro you farted?" he asked. BJ smiled, "let's do this," he said climbing out the car. "2 deep 2 Real"

It was pitch black on the streets. No Street lights, no nothing. Death in the air. As they approached the front door, BJ gripped the handle on the Mossberg extra tight. He could feel his adrenaline rushing. J-Note knocked and cocked the A.K. finger on the trigger as they heard footsteps come from inside the house. BJ took a deep breath, the door swung open and J-Note rushed the fat dude blazing, *[BAK . . . . BAK . . . . BAK . . . BAK . . . BAK . . . . BAK]*, J-Note let off shot after shot killing the fat dude instantly with two to the chest. Splattered blood was all over the wall. BJ didn't look at his body he just rushed in behind J-Note. Screaming, yelling, loud grunts, and gunshots! . . . *[BAK . . . BAK . . . BAK . . . BAK . . . BAK . . . BAK]* . . . J-Note wasn't shy with the A.K. he spit at least twenty rounds and still had thirty left. He dropped another dude and a third one ran to the backroom trying to get away. BJ chased him down, stopped and let off a round, *[BOOM]* . . . He missed and hit the wall. The dude struggled to get the window open and just as he saw the light BJ stopped around the corner and caught him with one foot out the window. *[BOOM],* The Mossberg roared and the slug caught the runner in the side. The impact knocked him out the window causing the window to shadow and blood splattered the wall. BJ ran to the window and pointed the Mossberg at the motionless body lying in the dark . . . *[BOOM]* . . . The blast lit up the darkness as the runner let out his last grunt of life. BJ ran back to the front room where he found J-Note loading up 20 gallons of codeine and ounces in the bag.

"You got the key? J-Note asked, stiffing the gallons in two big Nike gym bags. "What?" BJ asked confused. "The nigga you chased, that was Herb," J-Note explained. BJ ran back to the window, looked outside and climbed out. He wasn't too fond of dead bodies but he had to get the keys. Dead bodies and darkness creeped him out. He searched Herb's pockets, found the keys and climbed back through the window. He hit the front room, moved the dresser and pulled up an old rug where he found the safe in a hole under the wooden floor. He fumbled with the key as he heard sirens in the distance. He could hear J-Note yelling for him to hurry up. He popped the safe open and two stacks, about 25 G's. He thought to himself, he took a nigga's life for two stacks. He grabbed the money, stuffed it in the back pack he had on his back and jetted through the house. J-Note was already in the car had it running and waiting. BJ hopped in and they sped off turning on Green Span and made a right on Camp Wisdom. As they were leaving Wood Town, cops were headed to the bloodied, robbery, homicide scene.

*   *   *

Nephew and the twins were posted up on Kingsley in North Dallas at a Burger King. They were in

Nephew's Lincoln, rolling up some blunts about to hit up club GiGi's.

"Ay look out Malique, go in the trunk and grab that crown and coke," Nephew said as he put the finishing touches on his sweet. Tylique had just come out of Burger King with some cups and ice. "Say bro they say it's gone be crunk!" Tylique said putting fire to the blunt.

They were so caught up in doing what they were doing they didn't see a Cadillac creeping about ten yards away . . . . *TAT . . . TAT . . . . TAT . . . . TAT . . . . TAT . . . . TAT . . . . TAT . . . . TAT . . .*

The sound of a Tech-22 was spitting round after round at them. Yelling from the parking lot, windows shattering, Nephew and Tylique took cover; the only thing they could do . . . . *TAT . . . . TAT . . . . TAT . . . . TAT . . . . TAT . . . . TAT . . . . TAT . . . .* more shots. Nephew grabbed his 40 Cal, shots stopped. He peeped up and saw the lack backing up trying to get out the parking lot. In a rage Nephew hopped out and let his Cal do the talking . . . . *BAK . . . . BAK . . . . BAK . . . . BAK . . . BAK . . . . BAK . . . . BAK . . . . BAK . . . .* The 40 Cal barked and left the Lac riddled with broken windows and bullet holes as it sped down Kingsley.

"Marco! Marco!" Tylique yelled in a panicking voice. Nephew rushed to the back side of the car. Malique was laid out in his own blood gasping for air trying to hold on. Nephew panicked as he watched his lil bro slip into darkness. They loaded him up and sped all the way to Parkland Hospital which wasn't too far away.

Nephew called everybody and told them what happened. The Doctor told Nephew that Malique had a pulse and was in the surgery room. He caught a slug in the ankle, hip, top rib cage, shoulder, and one gazed his skull. All the damage was suffered on the right side of his body because of how he was standing when the bullets hit him.

It was four hours later and the room was packed with family and friends patiently waiting. The Doctor came out bloody, looking dazed. Expressions said a lot. The Doctor approached the large crowd looking sad and worn out. "Everyone, I'm Dr. McKenzie," he said removing his surgical mask and bloody gloves. "Who's the mother or guardian of the shot victim?" She confirmed that he could put the news out to everybody. "O.K. this is the deal, I know y'all have been out here for long hours and we did the best we could," The doctor said. When he said we did the best we could; everybody went into shock mode after hearing those fatal words. "Doc please just give it to us raw," KB said with his arms around his niece. "Alright, we were able to revive Malique after losing him twice but his condition is very vital. He has lost a lot of blood and the bullet that went through his shoulder stopped about three inches away from his heart. We didn't want to risk it and cut him open just yet because that would consist of more blood being lost so the bullet is at a stand still. Malique also lost one of his lungs and after surgery he slipped into a coma so I'm not making any promises. For immediate family, he's in I.C.U." After the doctor left everybody but the immediate family disappeared.

Nephew sat in daze thinking about how he was going to make his enemy pay. He was numb to anybody that tried to stop him.

*   *   *

Nephew stalked Lina's house for two days but came up disappointed. The only thing on his mind was catching up with Lonzo and leaving him in a pool of blood. He wasn't worried about Lonzo's weak crew cause neither one of them possessed the heart to retaliate on Nephew. But Nephew still didn't want to underestimate the power and abilities of his enemy. Out of Lonzo's crew, Nephew in some way respected Ra-Ra's gangsta but he was still no match for Nephew even in his prime.

Ra-Ra was six foot, caramel complexion, and loose cannon. He was Lonzo's muscle and hustle. If it wasn't for Ra-Ra's killer instinct, Lonzo's empire would have crumpled a long time ago. Ra-Ra handled every situation with extreme caution. He was known to jump the gun a lot of the times and reacting a little too quickly and early which earned him a handful of heads under his belt but he felt it was better safe than sorry. Lonzo's other two goons, BT and Crew, were flashy and flamboyant. They were known to get careless which led them to get stung a couple of times. BT really wasn't the street type but he was known to find connects and different types of licks to help keep Lonzo on top. Crew was the loud mouth of the click. He was a street nigga but he wasn't too smart. His weakness was females and he like to pull his stacks out and cap in front of a broad. Lonzo liked having him because of his personality and he was someone he could easily give orders to who would easily submit.

Nephew became restless, fired up his newly detailed Lincoln and left. He rode down Forest Lane and started thinking about Malique. He was the rowdy one of the twins. He was the rock star. All their lives they have been close. It wasn't anything Nephew wouldn't do for the twins. He dreaded anything happening to his lil bro cause he was sure he would be back in TDCJ with a couple of murder cases this time.

*   *   *

(*Cell phone ringing*) . . . "Give you the business," by Young Bird, going off. "Hello."

"Hey baby I got that info for you," the soft voice on the other line said. He got what he needed and ended his conversation with his female companion.

He rolled down Weaver St. and turned left on Clark Rd, heading to a neighborhood called the Planets. He turned right on Jupiter and rode the street until he reached Venus. The block was dark and looked peaceful so he rolled around the block twice scoping out the scene. He parked the stolen Lexus at the end of the street in front of a vacant duplex. Before he made his move he did a quick gun check. He was carrying two P.28 black and chrome ruggers; sixteen in the clip and one in the chamber. He had enough ammo to do the do. He made sure his vest was on tight and pulled his black ski mask over his face. After making sure everything was in tack, he clicked his guns together; "Let's do this shit nigga," he said to himself as his adrenaline pumped.

He got in front of the address Lisa gave him and checked the scene for a way in. He was just about to kick the door in when a female came walking out on her cell phone. He ducked behind some bushes and watched as the familiar female talked loudly on her phone. He crept from his spot and put the cold steel on the back of the girl's head. She jumped, startled as she realized what was pressured to her head. "Bitch if you yell or breathe too loud I'm knocking weave all over the yard," he whispered. "Now who all in the house?" he asked. "Bowie and J.J.," she answered quickly. "Please don't hurt me," she begged as tears rolled down her cheeks. "Shut up bitch and let's walk," BJ spat. He didn't have no sympathy for nobody just like nobody had any sympathy for him and his homeboy.

They walked through the front door and once BJ got around the wall he sprung into action. The first face he saw was J.J.'s. When J.J. saw the masked man he tried to react but it was too late. *BAK . . . . BAK . . . . BAK . . . BAK . . . BAK . . . . BAK*, brain fragments splattered on the wall as his chest leaked blood from hollow points that left holes the size of bagels in his plate. The girl screamed and BJ put one in her head putting her to sleep instantly. Bowie stepped out the bathroom and saw BJ making his way up the hall. BJ saw him and let off four shots *BAK . . . BAK . . . BAK . . . BAK . . .* Bowie ducked back in the bathroom awaiting his fate. He got caught slipping, shitting in the bathroom with no heat. "Come out nigga," BJ yelled. Bowie waited and waited until he heard the door crash in. He leaped at BJ and rushed him into the wall. BJ hit the wall hard and dropped one of his pistols. Bowie saw an opening and sprinted for the door. *BAK . . . . BAK . . .* BJ caught him once in the leg and in the shoulder. He scooped up his pistol and hovered over Bowie pulling his mask up revealing his mug. "Come one bro, don't do this man,"

Bowie said cowardly, pleading for his life. No words said, BJ let off eight rounds leaving Bowie lifeless.

Before he left, he ram shacked the place making it look like a robbery. He took a wad of money out of Bowie and J.J's pockets, leaving their pockets turned inside out and made his exit. Just as he made it to the corner of Jupiter about to turn on Clark, four police cars zoomed past. He sat back at the stop sign and hid behind the limo tint of the fancy luxury Lexus, undetected. He made a left on Clark, and then made a right on Parkerville. He rode all the way down Parkerville to a street called Main. He made a left on the back road and took Main across Beltline all the way to highway 67, leaving two dead snitches and a bitch behind.

*   *   *

Nephew was enjoying some much needed quality time with his main girl, Kayla. Their relationship was rocky due to Nephew's constantly running the streets and not only that, Nephew's hotline cell phone stayed ringing through the wee hours of the night. One night while he was gone off that syrup and weed, his cell phone was going off. Kayla answered and was displeased when she heard another female's voice. She made it known she was Nephew's wifey and hung the phone up. That type of shit happened couple of times but she never said anything to Nephew until now. She appreciated everything Nephew did for her but she refused to continue to be disrespected after she had been so loyal to him.

After a heated argument and Nephew's promise to chill, Kayla found herself enjoying some of the best oral sex she ever had. Nephew sucked on her clitoris like his life depended on it. He slid his middle finger in her cotton candy, making circular motions. His gentle touch stimulated juices from her pretty light brown pussy lips. Nephew locked every drop. She arched her back and moved her hips in coordination with his finger and tongue. Kayla sucked her bottom lip and grabbed Nephew's head as he devoured her flesh. Her insides were on fire as her fluids escaped her middle. She hissed and moaned as Nephew licked between her slit. With his index finger and thumb, he gently squeezed her clitoris as licked up her honey. Kayla started squirming, trying to get away as Nephew worked her G-spot. He picked her up and flipped her upside down, forcing her into the 69 position. "Don't drop me boy," Kayla pleaded as she wrapped her legs around Nephew's neck. "Don't worry baby, I got you," he said, holding her 5 foot 3 frame with ease. Kayla took Nephew in her mouth and licked circles around the head of his piece. As she held the back of his thighs, she slowly made love to his candy stick by working her mouth and neck. She tightened her jaws and tried to suck the life out of Nephew. She knew she was getting down because his knees buckled as pleasure ran through him. She was bobbing fast as if she was bobbing for apples; if so she would have won first place. "sssss . . . shit girl! You gone make me drop you." Kayla continued bobbing and sucking as she felt his dick expand in her mouth. Nephew sucked and licked on Kayla's clit as he felt her tense up, knowing she was close to a climax. The only sound in the room was that of Chris Brown's "Take You Down" along with all the sucking, slurping, moaning, and groaning as they both reached their peak; neither stopped as they received each other's honey.

Nephew flipped Kayla back on her feet and she stumbled a bit from being light headed. She smiled as Nephew stepped back toward the bed admiring her physique. She was a perfect petite 32C-24-38 and had a golden brown complexion that represented her Puerto Rican and African-America bloodline. She kind of reminded you of the likes of Joy Bryant, the female that played 50 Cent's baby mama in "Get Rich or Die Trying."

Nephew laid on his back as she crawled her small framed on top of him and straddled his middle. She grabbed the base of his dick and directed him to her middle. She continued to hold it as the head slipped in her opening. Kayla worked her hips in a circular motion teasing him. He moaned and she smiled as they locked eyes. She moved her hand and placed them on his chest as she slid all the way down to the base. She could fill his swollen dick fill her pussy. She closed her eyes and just sat on it before she began moving. Nephew massaged her perky nipples as he felt his head touch the top of her pussy. She threw her head back and started going in slow circles as his dick touched every inch of her tight pusst. Kayla started rocking back and forth as they gazed in each other's eyes. "Mmm . . . . sssss," she moaned as her she leaned her head forwarded enjoying the pleasure. She leaned all the way forward as Nephew wrapped his hands around her. She bounced up and down on his dick, base to base. "Aww . . . fuck," she moaned as she buried her face in Nephew's chest. He started meeting her thrust as she sat up a little, allowing him to work his bottom. She started coming down harder as her insides boiled. Nephew felt he was about to climax and started tossing his hips faster, bashing in her walls. Kayla cried out as her muscles tightened up. She dropped down taking him all the way in as she grinded him until she started to cum. "Ohh . . .God . . .Yesss," she moaned. Nephew put his hands around her hips and helped her pick up speed as he closed his eyes and filled her jar with his honey. Kayla pressed down harder making her clit rub his pelvis as her pussy swallowed his seeds. She exploded again and then rested on his chest as they both tried to catch their breaths. Nephew felt Kayla's juices run between his thighs. He stroked her wavy hair as she laid there still in an orgasmic daze.

"You straight baby girl?" he asked as he rubbed her back. She looked up and smiled, "yeah I'm good boo," she replied as she kissed his lips and climbed off of him and headed to the bathroom. Nephew watched her glistening, naked body disappear in the bathroom. She came back with a towel and wiped him down. He pulled her in the bed and wrapped her in his long arms. "You know I love you Kayla," he said softly. "No matter what I do in them streets, it's all about you; number one. It's a fact that bitches know who my queen is, so don't ever forget that. You are special to me and you're an important piece to my life," he said looking in her green eyes. Kayla nodded her head as a tear fell from her eyes. "Marco, I'm dangerously in love with you. Don't forget that daddy. Just be more discrete bout yo business," she said softly. They cuddled in each other's arms and feel into a deep sleep, exhausted.

*　　*　　*

CHAPTER 13

It was the beginning of December and Malique was still in a coma. Nephew was unsuccessful in locating Lonzo or anybody from his crew. Nephew even went as far as beating Lina down. Within the months his family took Lina to court and got custody of his son. Business was still good with the crew. They managed to run through the 50 pounds of Hydro and 1000 X-pills. Pedro was more than happy to double the product and drop their prices.

KB was on the road every other weekend dropping off products to Chuck and James. KB was pleased that they didn't have to result to robbing anybody. KB and Profit ran into each other on occasions but it wasn't any beef. KB got word that Profit and his crew was talking down on him and his people and they were planning to make a move. KB fought with himself everyday to not get the info on Profit and his big move. The shit was eating at him because he knew if it was that big of a move then it would surely benefit him and his crew.

BJ had been going back to forth to court with Dam-Dam's family showing his best friend some support. The D.A. didn't have much of a case but Dam and his family was still reluctant of going to trial. Many of times BJ would lace Dam-Dam up on how crooked the system worked. Even though they didn't have much of anything but being that he was a young dude being accused of capital murder, the jury would still sentence him to life. Dam-Dam and his lawyer went ahead and accepted a plea bargain of 10 years in T.D.C.J. The D.A. dropped the capital charge to second degree murder so Dam-Dam signed the papers. Due to the fact that he had two years back time in the county, he was eligible for parole in another three years. All worked out well.

It was a gray and breezy Sunday, BJ and Tara were coming from a soul food restaurant, Sweet Georgia Brown. They were cruising down Ledbetter when they got caught at red light on Marsailis. "Baby did you enjoy the service," Tara asked. BJ just looked at her and smiled. He wasn't too fond of doing dirt Monday through Saturday, the putting up a front on Sunday. He was reared to be a God fearing man but he wasn't spiritual. He was based his life mainly on a reality basis and reality was that extreme things happened whether you were in church or not. "Don't be like that," Tara said as she rolled her eyes at him. "I'm just saying baby; I be out here 24/7 doing dirt. I don't want to be no hypocrite," he explained. "But I did enjoy going with you though," he said smiling and grabbing her hand. Tara leaned over and kissed him. When she opened her eyes they went buck as she notices the barrel of two guns being pointed their way. BJ saw her expression and turned to see two dudes on a black and red R1. "Baby get down!" he yelled. But it

was too late . . . . BAK . . . BAK . . . BAK . . . BAK . . .
BAK . . . BAK . . . BAK . . . BAK . . . BAK.

The sound of the two 40 cals roared as BJ floored the chevy, swerving. He was ducked in his seat so by the time he lifted his head, it was too late. He had smashed into a light pole and everything went black.

*   *   *

BJ woke up in confused with a massive headache. His vision was blurry and he didn't understand what was going on. He closed his eyes over and over in an attempt to focus them. (beep . . . beep . . . beep . . . beep), he heard the sounds of a heart monitor and looked to his right. He sat up as things became clearer. Hospital? His thoughts were roaming. He got dizzy and hot all of a sudden and laid back down and closed his eyes.

"Baby get down!" he heard himself yelling in the darkness . . . BAK . . . BAK . . . BAK . . . BAK . . . BAK . . . BAK . . . BAK . . . BAK. He heard gunshots, 20 rounds, but he didn't see anything. He heard a female screaming and could see her face. Tara. (ssskkkkkiiirrrrtttt), the sounds of tires screeching as he peeled off. More shots, more screaming, BAM! A crash and everything went black again. He saw the wreck.

Things were starting to make sense now. It was clear to him what happened. His eyes flew open as he sat straight up in the hospital bed. "Tara!" he yelled as he ripped tubes out of his nose and arms. He sung his legs around and tried to stand up only to lose his balance. Head throbbing, nose running, eyes watering with blood; he panicked trying to make it to Tara. A Doctor and nurse ran into the room and tried to get him back in bed. He struggled, crying "I gotta help my girl," he said delusional. "Mr. Johnson, you need to lay back down," the tall doctor said. "I can't. Got to get to Tara," he said as he tried to break away from the doctor. As weak as he was, he could not break free from the strong hold of the doctor. He finally gave up and layid down. The nurse cleared his nose and put an ice pack on his head to cool him down. He drifted off, closed his eyes and welcomed darkness again.

*　　*　　*

When BJ opened his eyes again he saw his mama, Tara's mama, his sister, and KB in the room. The tears were in the ladies' eyes and grief on his homeboy's face. He laid there confused as to why they were all crying, was he dead? He reached out to touch his mama and she reached back. Their hands locked together and he could feel her flesh. She bent over, kissed him and he tried to smile because he knew at that point he was still alive. He spoke in a raspy voice, "where Tara?" he asked. More tears rolled from the ladies' eyes. "Mama what's up? Mrs. Green. Somebody talk to me?" he said in a weak, worn tone. "His mama spoke up. "Baby, Tara died," she answered as both of the mothers hugged. Tears fell from his eyes. He closed them and saw Tara's face bleeding, swollen, as she laid in the passenger's side of his Caprice; lifeless and bloody with glass in her lap. He reached over and touched her face, wiping away blood that was dripping down the side of her face. Darkness.

That night after everybody left his room, he looked out of his window at the city as the rain fell just like tears that were rolling off his cheek. He thought about all the dirt he did and the lives he took. Was this God's way of paying him back for his counts of murder? Was God trying to get his attention? Why Tara? His heart grew cold and he became numb as he looked over the city where those responsible were lurking. He hated it for his unknown assassins because he wasn't going to rest until they were dead. He kept the streets in the streets, never fucked with anyone's family. Now his enemies made business personal.

*   *   *

Tara's funeral was very emotional for everyone. It was a dark and gloomy day and the funeral was set. The atmosphere was full of nothing but loud and hard cries. After the burial, BJ assured her brothers he was going to avenge her death until his death. Everything was understood between the families. Out of pure revenge he downed two of Bowie's protégés, Jamal and Dre. They were dead before Tara's dirt dried. He felt it was a safe move being that he was getting word that they suspected him in the murder of Bowie and J.J.so his motive for killing them was covered.

*   *   *

The New Years rolled around and BJ celebrated it with his crew; Lisa, Nina, Kitty, Jayla, Yasmin and other females. KB brought Stacy and Nephew brought his main girl Kayla. BJ decided to use his condo for a New

Year's party because it was spacious. He wasn't too worried about neighbors because he had his spot sound proofed. Everybody was dancing and having a good time drinking, smoking, and freaking. Tara was heavy on his mind but he laid his emotions to the side and tried to have a good time. "Say Bam, where that bowl of kill at?" BJ yelled over the music. Bam was ducked off in the corner getting a lap dance from Yasmin and grinning from ear to ear. "That nigga Guillotine took it in the game room," Bam said, waving BJ off. BJ made his way to the game room and walked in on Guillotine, Velt, and LD getting it in with Nina and two more of Nina's Latina friends. Nina was between LD's legs giving him some lip service while Guillotine and Velt had the other two beauties eating each other out. BJ stood and watched the girl on girl action. "Say bro this party is what's up!" Velt yelled as he tossed back the rest of his Bud Ice. "I'm glad you niggas having fun but where the weed at?" BJ asked. Velt pointed him in the direction of the mini wet bar where he saw the bowl of half empty good. "Damn nigga I know y'all ain't smoking like that," BJ said as he held the bowl up. "Nigga we ain't the only ones smoking," Velt said, holding up an El Producto full of weed. "Happy New Year's mothafuckas," BJ said smiling. They nodded and turned their attention back to the two Latino's that were pleasing each other. BJ stood there for a minute and admired the two beautiful, curvaceous women. One of them looked like Vida Guerrera and the other one looked like the chic from Rush Hour 2, Roselyn Sanchez.

As he made his exit, he could see the silhouette of a female frame standing in the doorway of his guestroom. As he was trying to make sense of who it was, she stepped out of the shadow into the light. "What's up boo?" the soft voice asked. He smiled, "Lisa, you a trip," he said examining her body. She was looking good in her strapless black Donna Karen skirt with some black three inch open toe pumps by Giovanni. The skirt complimented her every curve. BJ licked his lips, "Tara ain't been in the dirt 30 days and you already tryna seduce a nigga," he said smiling. "Naw it ain't like that," she said strutting over to him with her model walk, throwing her arms around his neck while he rubbed her ass. "What it's like then?" he asked, squeezing her soft apple bottom. "I respect your girl and I respect you too daddy, but you can't mourn forever," she said looking into his eyes. BJ held her gaze and looked deep into her grey eyes. She was right, he couldn't mourn forever and he still had to live his life. He loved Tara deeply and knew that he always would, but he had to move on and there was no other woman to do it with other than Lisa. She had proven her loyalty and showed him that she was down for him. Not only that, she knew how to keep him pleased.

BJ leaned in and they shared one of the most passionate kisses that they have ever shared with each other. Lisa was pleased to now be crowned BJ's main girl. She was well satisfied after all the time she put into him. Now, it has finally paid off but out of respect for Tara, she wanted to give him time to get over his loss. At the same time she didn't want to risk another female playing the role she deserved to be in. She loved him just that much.

*   *   *

CHAPTER 14

KB secluded himself from everyone as he took the time he needed to collect the information to move in on Profit. Word got back to KB that once Profit made this major move, he was going to eliminate KB and his crew. He also got a tip that Profit put a price on Baby Jay's head to get him out of the area because he knew Baby Jay was coming with cheaper prices and was sewing up some major spots in Highland Hills. Profit took that as a sign of disrespect because everybody knew he had Highland Hills on lock and that was his hood. With Baby Jay making moves in the area, Profit felt like it was making him look weak to let a nigga that was not part of the hood sew the bitch up.

KB purposely kept that info from BJ because he knew with everything BJ was going through that he was a loose cannon and he wouldn't waste any time killing Profit which in turn would mess up KB's plan. KB thought out his master plan and looked it over as he smoked on a hydro blunt. He smiled to himself at the thought of how things would be if everything went as planned.

*　　*　　*

KB pulled up to V.I.P. parking in his money green Lexus and saw BJ's bloody BMW and Nephew's Escalade parked in valet parking. He was meeting them at Club Robby's to discuss his plan and to holla at Tessca. Tessca was a major, major factor in Dallas because she knew people that knew people that knew people. Dame and Robby left her and her sister-n-law, Megan, stacked. Tessca was Robby's older sister and when Robby and Dame met their unfortunate end, she took over the club and also blew up in the drug trafficking game thanks to her homeboy Ghetto Bill and some associates that Megan knew from her native hometown, Arkansas. One of her brothers, Ron, got out the Feds and didn't waste no time blowing back up. KB met Tessca through BJ. BJ was an associate of Robby and Dame and before he caught his case, him and Dam-Dam use to do small favors for Tessca.

KB paid his cash and stepped through the door looking like the player of the year. He was rocking a beige and cream Giorgio Armani, short sleeve button down shirt, some cream Giorgio Armani slacks, and topped it off with his cream Gators. He accented his outfit with an iced out watch, bracelet, and chain which made him stand out even more. He made his way into the ballroom and saw all kinds of naked and half naked exotic foreign dancers. Club Robby's wasn't your average strip joint. It was very sophisticated and classy. The atmosphere was chill and warming. Club Robby's hosted many celebrity parties, bachelor parties, release parties, and many other types of main events. It was a highly recommended club throughout the states.

KB scanned the club for his peeps but didn't see BJ or Nephew. He turned around when he heard a female's voice call his name, landing his eyes on a beautiful site. "Megan, what's up lil mama?" he said, giving her a hug. "Ain't too much, where you been hiding at? Looking like a million bucks," she said smiling. "Shit I've been on it, trying to reach Hollywood status, he said smiling. "Boy you crazy." "Ay, have you seen BJ?" he asked. "Yeah he upstairs in VIP," she said pointing at the stairs that led to about six secluded VIP rooms. "If Tessca got time, tell her to come fuck with me, it's urgent," KB said as they parted ways. He walked through the spacious club and up the stairs towards the VIP rooms.

The rooms looked over the club and each room had its own privacy. You could see out the tinted windows but no one could see in. Each room consisted of three round tables and three black leather couches that could hold up to four people. To get a VIP room it cost $3,500, straight baller prices. KB walked in the room and saw BJ and Nephew getting served with some lap dances by two fine dancers named Obsession and Cherish.

Obsession was a red skin Brazilian beauty. She had short wavy hair that stopped at her neck. She possessed some deep brown eyes, full cheek bones, and some pretty caramel lips. She stood 5 foot 10 inches with some 32D cups, a 26 inch waist line, and a firm 45 inch ass. Cherish was a dark skinned, Kingston African Queen. Her hair hung in thick braids that went down to her butt. She looked like the porn star, Jada Fire. She stood 5'11 and possessed very nice round 36DD cups, a 28 inch waist line, and 54 inch beach ball booty. Everything about her said foreign; she was an exotic Amazon.

When KB stepped in the room BJ and Nephew dismissed the ladies. BJ tucked his erection in his jeans and zipped his pants up. He pulled his piece out so he could get the full feeling of his lap dance. "You freaky lil bastard," KB said smiling and dapping BJ and Nephew up. "Man that bitch Cherish got a super fat pussy. Her lips fat as the world," BJ said while they all laughed as his stupid ass. "Don't tell me you gone gal her too," Nephew said cutting his eye at KB. BJ saw them looking at him trying to hold their laughs in. He looked at them and tipped his drink up. "Fuck y'all, she too big for me anyway; bitch will probably whoop a nigga," he said. They all laughed because she did look like a giant compared to BJ's 5'8 frame.

They chatted and mingled as KB proceeded to tell them about the lick he had been putting together. After he gave them the run down, leaving nothing out, BJ and Nephew agreed and voted themselves in on the cash cow. KB made his exit and headed for Tessca's office, while BJ indulged in some foreign sex with Cherish. Nephew went down stairs to give BJ some privacy and sat in front of the stage while another foreign dancer named Thames, from London did her thing. She had to be the biggest, finest white girl on earth. She was at least 6'2 with long blonde hair and brown streaks. She had eyes like Angelina Jolie and lips that resembled a mixture of both Angelina and Jessica Alba. Her breasts were a firm 34DDD and she had a 28 inch waist line. She had a 52 inch mountain ass carried by her voluptuous hips. Her thighs were nice and thick and she was rocking some 6 inch hills that accented her sexy legs.

KB was sitting in Tessca's office engaging in some small talk. He had never been in her office before. It was decked out nice like a living room. It had two leather couches, mini wet bar and family pictures on the wall. Behind her were two human size photos of Robby and Dame. He looked at Robby's picture and noticed how much he resembled BJ. The only difference was BJ was more buff. He figured maybe that was why Tessca liked BJ so much was because he looked like her brother.

"So what's up KB, what did you wanna holla at me about?" She asked. "I'm about to get my hands on some major weight and soon as I touch it I'm gone need to get rid of it and I know you're in a position to help a brother on the rise," KB explained. "Alright, when you get yo hands on it come fuck with me," Tessca said seriously. KB smiled, all he needed to do now was get the work.

*   *   *

Nephew was still determined to bring Lonzo out of hiding. He stalked North Dallas but nothing ever transpired. That following night, he and LD were sitting across the street in front of a rim shop as they watched BT and Crew swing through the parking lot of Rack Daddy's. Their target was easy being that they were in a maroon Lincoln Navigator. The club had just let out and cars were everywhere. They followed the 04 Navigator to the Denny's up the street off I-20 and Cockrell Hill. The Navigator parked and the two hopped out and headed in the restaurant. Nephew parked where no one could see his car and headed for the front door of Denny's. He wanted to walk up in that bitch masked up and fire them niggas up but he stuck to the script that LD proposed.

LD was a thorough street nigga and he was a massive thinker. Nephew trusted the nigga with his life because he knew LD was gone hold it down no matter what they were up against. Nephew watched from a distance as BT and Crew were seated in a booth toward the back of the restaurant, accompanied by two female companions. Nephew sat at the bar and slurped on a strawberry shake as he watched his prey socialize like things were all good. He paid for his drink and made his way over to their table. If he was a fool he could have pulled both of his straps off his hip and knocked them off on the spot. He made it over to their table and BT and Crew finally saw him standing over them. All talking ceased and smiles turned into frowns as they looked in the eyes of their hunter. The girls sensed trouble and tried to scoot out of the booth.

Nephew lifted up his shirt and showed the butt of one his Glock .380's, "Sit y'all asses down," he ordered them. The females scooted back in their seats and sat quietly waiting for the situation to play out. "Scoot your fine ass over and let me sit down," he said to one of the girls. She was a pretty light skin girl that looked like Zoe Saldana in the face. "What's up fellas, it's been a minute," Nephew said smiling as he grabbed some fries off one of the girl's plate and stuck them in his mouth. BT and Crew just stared at him. "Damn what's up, cat got y'all tongues?" Nephew asked as he picked up the cheeseburger sitting on the plate in front of him and took a bite. He turned toward "Zoe Saldana" and stuck his hand out. "Hey Ms. Lady, I'm Nephew, what's yo name?" he said like shit was cool.

She looked at BT and Crew and then at her home girl as they all looked terrified. "I'm Tiffany," she answered, shaking his hand. "Ay ladies, it's cool y'all don't have to be sced of a nigga. And what are y'alls name," he asked the other two, showing his diamonds." They looked at each other, "I'm Bre-Bre," one answered, "and I'm LaNay," the other replied. "Cool, cool. Y'all are some pretty ass chics, what y'all doing with dead beat ass niggas?" he asked. Bre Bre shrugged her shoulders, "nothing just chillin." Nephew pulled out a real fat wad of money, nothing but $100 bills. "Tiffany, I really want to get to know you, huh? Fuck with a real nigga. These boys gone get y'all hurt out here. Me and some homeys gotta suite downtown. It's one of my nigga's birthday so what's up y'all wanna roll?" he asked, smooth smiling at all of them. The girls looked at each other and nodded in approval. "Yeah its cool," LaNay answered, thinking about the money Nephew flashed. Nephew turned his attention toward BT and Crew, "where ya boy Lonzo at?" "Man fuck you nigga! Who you thank you tryna hoe up in this bitch?" Crew asked raising his voice. "Nigga you better lower yo voice," Nephew said, frowning hard. "I just wanted y'all to meet y'alls maker. You can thank Lonzo for that," he said, standing up as he threw $200 on the table. "Ladies what y'all gone do? Bar-B-Que or mildew? These dudes night is officially over," he said smiling.

The girls grabbed their purses and stood next to Nephew. He threw his arms around Tiffany and they made their exit. "Where y'all car at?" he asked. "We caught the bus from The Harbors," Tiffany answered. She was still a little timid about the situation. He shook his head and they followed him to his car. When they saw how he was rolling, they looked at each other and smiled in approval. When Nephew saw that LD was not in the car, he knew he had made his move. "Ladies we'll be heading out in a minute, I'm waiting for the birthday boy. Do y'all smoke weed?" He asked, pulling out a bag of Hydro. Bre-Bre and LaNay smiled at each other, "Hell yea we smoke, what's up?" Bre-Bre said. Nephew tossed her the fat ounce of dro bag from his glove compartment along with some sweets.

*　　*　　*

Meanwhile . . . . (**BT & Crew**)

"Man we need to get at Lonzo so we can gone and take care of that fool," BT said as they walked out the restaurant. "Don't trip my nigga, for now its S.O.S. he said, climbing in the passenger's side of the Navigator. BT looked at him, "Bitch why you didn't lock the doors? You always do that shit," he said, hopping in the driver seat. "Nigga shut up, don't nobody want th . . . ." *(BAK . . . . BAK);* the sounds of the gun and the sight of BT's brains on the dash stopped him mid sentence. Before he could do anything he was looking down the barrel of a chrome .38 Special. It wasn't anything he could do but accept what was about to happen. Fuck it; it was part of the game. "It's too late to turn back the hands of time. What's up?" Crew said boldly. The gunman smiled and dumped three hallows in the loud mouth. He looked around before hopping out the Navigator and made his exit. He tucked the guns and walked around the building to Nephew's car.

Nephew listened for the muffled sound of the .38's going to work. He was pleased when he heard two, then three more shots. A minute later LD was walking around the corner. He opened the door to some beautiful faces and the smell of chronic. "Happy birthday!" Nephew said, smiling with the girls following suit. LD smiled and went with the program even though his birthday was four months away.

*   *   *

CHAPTER 15

KB had everyone in position. The drop was at an old warehouse out in Wilmer Hutchins, in the middle of nowhere. The drop wasn't until 9:30 but KB had everyone situated before time. Bam was on the roof with an AR-15 extended clip. From his angle he could cover the whole warehouse floor undetected. LD, Marcus, and Velt covered the back. LD and Marcus was strapped with Russian AK 47's with 100 round Tommy drums. Velt had a 50 round sub-machine gun, with two extra clips and a silencer. J-Note and George held the front down with two 100 round MP 5's, both had silencers. They were to take out both the guards that would be holding the front door. KB, BJ, and Guillotine were in different corners of the warehouse. The exchange spot was set up and KB was secure. KB had everything down packed; I's dotted and T's crossed. He told his team they had to be on point and no slip ups. With himself, Guillotine, LD, Bam, and George in the line up, he was confident in his plan. He was grateful to have so many sharp shooters on his squad. He learned that Bam and George did about three years together in the military before being discharged for behavioral problems. They both served as snipers and took pride in their abilities. Guillotine and LD were just two niggas that were infatuated with guns. They admired all guns, from the smallest to the biggest. LD was the reason they were sitting on so much artillery.

KB was posted where he could see Bam. They had already knocked glass from the roof so that Bam could have a clear shot at his target. His mission was to clear out all the big guns. KB, Nephew, Guillotine, and BJ would do the floor work. At about 9:20, two black 2006 Hummer 3's pulled up in front of the warehouse. Four big muscular bound dudes strapped with M 16 rifles hopped out the back. Two took up the front and two to the back. Once they were in position, two Cubans and two guards hopped out the front Hummer. Each Cuban had two brief cases in hand and proceeded into the warehouse to sit things up. Right at 9:35 Profit and two of his goons, Flip and Dooley, pulled up in one of his black Lexus. They hopped out engaging in conversation; laughing, talking and smiling. Dooley was carrying two Gucci bags as they entered the warehouse and proceeded to swap it out. Profit shook hands with the two Cubans that were referred by Diaz. "My friend, it's good to see you," the shorter of the two said, smiling. "I'm glad that we could do business. I'm very honored to be in your presence and I've heard a lot about you from my great friend Diaz Mercardo," Profit said. KB sat back in the dark and listened to the conversation. He was surprised to hear that the same connect he was getting his birds from was Profit's connect too.

J-Note and George made their move from both sides of the front. George motioned for J-Note to strike.

J-Note aimed and hit the guard on the left with three shots. The guard grunted and crumbled to the ground. The other guard turned and tried to assist his partner but was met with five hot slugs, dropping him instantly. J-Note went and jumped in one of the Hummers and turned it around to face the street, then did the other the same way. He then sliced the tires on the Lexus just in case Profit somehow managed to get away.

LD checked his watch and saw it was ten minutes after their arrival. It was striking time. He motioned for Velt to do his and one by one he dropped both guards with a barrage of slugs from the sub-machine, quiet as kept. KB checked his watch and figured the guards should be part of the past by now. Profit and the Cubans were wrapping things up. He motioned for Bam to take out the guard at the back door. Bam popped his neck and focused on the guard through his scope. "Say good night mothafucka," Bam said as he pulled the trigger on the AR-15, sounding off and hitting the guard in the head. The sound made everybody turn around and draw down. The guard from the front raised his M-16 and pointed it in the direction from where the shot came. Guillotine came up from his spot and let the street sweeper go to work. The guard from the front was sent flying across the warehouse from the impact of the sweeper. "Ambush! Ambush!" one of the Cubans yelled, pulling out two pistols and shooting with no control. His partner follow suit and within seconds the warehouse was filled with gunshots.

Profit made his way to the money and drugs while his goons covered him. Dooley grabbed the bags of money and proceeded to cover Profit as Flip grabbed two of the brief cases. KB ducked behind a crate and aimed his pistol at Flip. *BAK . . . BAK . . . BAK . . . BAK . . . BAK . . . BAK.* Flip's chest exploded from the slugs of the .45 Dessert Eagle. He folded right where he was standing with blood leaking out of four fresh holes. BJ ducked and let off rounds as bullets flew by his head. *BAK . . . BAK . . . BAK . . . BAK . . .* He downed one of the Cubans running his way; the other one saw his partner crumble to the floor and went into a rage. He scooped up one of the dead guard's M-16 and started bucking wildly. "Ahhhhhh," he yelled as he fired off shots emptying the gun.

Profit and Dooley were at the door when Dooley caught two slugs from the M-16. Profit grabbed one of the Gucci bags that had two brief cases inside. KB saw him getting away, *BAK . . . BAK . . . BAK . . .* Profit caught a slug in his shoulder and went down, dropping the merchandise and money. He grabbed his pistol and ran through the front. Luckily J-Note and George went to the back.

Profit ran for his Lexus, hopped in, and peeled off only to find out the tires were flat. He continued to punch the Lexus down the side service road, wondering how everything went wrong. His mind was trying to put things in perspective. Whoever put the hit together was well organized. The average street nigga couldn't have pulled off something like that. It took weeks and weeks of planning. Not only did they have the place mapped but they obviously knew what time the drop was going to take place because they had gunmen inside the warehouse ducked off. Whoever it was had to have some inside information. Profit's mind instantly went to Diaz, his long time connect. He was the only one aware of the drop and knew everything; from the connect, to the time, down to knowing all about the spot. Never in his life was Profit so vulnerable. He was so anxious to make a major move that he failed to look into it more than what he did. Now it cost him half million of hard earned dirty money.

KB got his team, money, and merchandise and loaded up in both the hummers as he made his way down I-30. Mission accomplished. Except for the fact they somehow let Profit get away. That wasn't really a major issue but he knew him and his crew would have to be on their P's and Q's. KB gave Tessca a call and forty five minutes later he was pulling up in front of her spot with 80 Kilo's of pure cocaine. He ordered his crew to park the Hummers and chill until he returned. He was let in by the guards and marched straight to Tessca's office.

"Hey KB, this my people Ghetto Bill," she said. They exchanged greetings and got right down to business. "So I see you in all black, thangs straight?" Tessca asked out of concern. KB smiled, "yeah! You know how we rock; if thangs wasn't straight I wouldn't be here." "Right on," Tessca said. "What the run on forty?" she asked. "3.5," KB answered. "Tessca and Ghetto looked at each other and smiled, "man this is better than pussy," Ghetto said, smiling. After they made the transaction KB assured Tessca that he would stay in touch. He walked out of Club Robby's $700,000 richer.

*   *   *

CHAPTER 16

After busting the money down ten ways, everyone was $120,000 richer. KB, BJ, and Nephew got on I-45S and took the other twenty birds to James and Chuck in Houston. They agreed to break the birds down and go gram for gram. James was in a position on the sunny south side to triple the profit. Chuck and his little bro had the whole 44acres of Holmes area sewed up. James managed to sting the block or anybody inquiring for 25G/brick. He had some reliable niggas that ran spots for him rock for rock. It would take two weeks at the most to get rid of the products.

KB, BJ, and Nephew decided to get a three bedroom apartment on the Southwest side of Houston just to lay low for a while. They made the necessary calls to their people informing them that things were gravy. First it was the girlfriends; Stacy wasn't tripping, she had a couple of parties she had to host being that she was the "Digital Dime Piece" of the year. She was popular on Myspace and many other networking websites. She also made a name for herself with different clubs in Miami, Atlanta, Chicago, New York, and L.A. All of the clubs wanted this popular urban model to host parties at their club.

Nephew assured his girl Kayla all was well and that he would be back on the scene in a couple of months. Kayla was content with her man being gone because she had more than enough to keep her busy at her brother's club. "Connections" was also one of the hottest dance clubs in the metroplex so it was all good in her world. With all that was going on they needed some space anyway.

BJ had a little trouble with Lisa because she wanted to be with her man so bad. Once BJ assured her that he was coming back she calmed down. BJ meant everything to Lisa and her daughter. Not just because he was breaking bread but he and Lizzarha had formed a tight bond. He made things family oriented when he dealt with them. Lisa loved him for doing what no other man, including her baby daddy, would do.

The trio knew enough people in H-Town to show them around the city. One day they were chilling on the Southside when BJ recognized one of his favorite rappers coming out of the Late DJ Screw's screw shop. "Pull over nigga," BJ said excitedly as he pointed to the screw shop. KB whipped the black rented Benz in the parking lot and parked next to a white Expedition wrapped with A.B.N. stitches. "Aw nigga you boppin now," KB said smiling, knowing that Z-Ro was BJ's favorite down south rapper. "I don't give a damn," he said smiling and showing his grill as he hopped out the back seat. Z-Ro was one of Houston's finest rappers. He was down with the late DJ Screw's crew known as the "Screwed Up Click," *S.U.C.* BJ grew up listening to the crew; Big Moe, Lil KeKe, Big Hawk, Fat Pat, Big Dokey, Z-Ro, Lil Flip and many more.

BJ walked up to him like a groupie and smiled. Z-Ro looked him over for a minute before BJ broke the silence. "Damn man I finally get to meet you face to face. Bro I been bumping you since 97,98. You my favorite rapper dude." They embraced and Z-Ro smiled showing his iced out grill. "Hey homey I appreciate the love G. I'm always honored to meet a true fan homey so here's an invite to my show tonight. Me, Trae, and the whole Gorilla Mobb fam gone be present," Z-Ro said as he handed BJ the invite flyer. BJ took off his plain white T and handed it to Z-Ro, "hey do you mind signing this? No homo but I'm a G for you and that nigga Trae. Y'all the truth in the booth," he said hyped up. Z-Ro laughed and called Trae over. BJ shook hands with the asshole by nature and both Trae and Z-RO signed the T-shirt. BJ was really star struck when he made it back to the car.

"Damn dawg you shoulda let the nigga sign yo ass cheek," KB said as him and Nephew burst into laughter. "Fuck y'all nigga!" I've been jamming Ro for years and I ain't never met dude in person. I had to show him some love," BJ explained as he sipped his drank. "But damn bro you took ya shirt off and everything showing off that hairy ass chest, you shoulda gave him a kiss on the cheek before you left," Nephew added. "I got some hairy ass cheeks you and ya uncle can kiss. Now pass the sweet."

*   *   *

PROFIT:

A month and a half has passed since Profit took that major lost in the streets. He was on his last leg in the game due to the lick. Profit, Bren, Creep, and Barry went on a robbing rampage to get their establishment back together. He was at war with Pedro Mercardo after him and his small crew ran up in Diaz's restaurant and killed him along with three of his main runners. After Profit took a lost, Diaz started handling him like a peon, giving him scraps. Diaz had cut Profit off because he said him and his crew were hot boys in the streets. This added to Profit's suspicion that Diaz had something to do with the hit since Diaz never took a lost or slowed down. From his understanding, The Cubans were Diaz's main connect and with them being dead he figured Diaz would be in a bad position. Profit also got word from the streets that the hit came from "*The Man*." Being that Diaz was a major important player in the game, he figured he was "*The Man*" so . . . .

Profit also heard that KB and his lame crew was scoring from Diaz. The info he received told him that KB dealt strongly with Diaz's nephew, Pedro. Pedro kicked it with him and his crew like they were old high school buddies or some shit. Profit envied the connection KB and Pedro had so he figured if they were buddies the KB and his crew were rolling in dough. Shit was getting thick for him and his people so he had to think of something quick.

* * *

Nephew received a call a few weeks ago telling him that Malique was back. He explained to his bro what was going on and assured him that they would be showing their faces in a couple of weeks. He was laid out across chuck's couch when his cell phone started going off. He was exhausted from the previous night. Him, BJ, Chuck's little brother Big, and D-Redd enjoyed a night at one of the Northside's local strip joints. Big and D-Redd were some more dudes that BJ, Nephew, and KB knew from the unit they were on. The night was filled with Codeine and Sprite, X-pills, weed, liquor and sex. So Nephew was trying to catch up on some much needed sleep but his damn cell phone kept ringing. He flipped it open, "Man what's up?" he asked in an aggravated tone. "Damn did I catch you at a bad time?" the soft voice asked. "Naw who is this?" "This Tiffany, you remember me?" she asked smiling. Nephew sat straight up; not only did he remember her but he kicked himself for not keeping in contact with the super head. She was the only girl he knew that could make a nigga nut in five minutes by sucking his dick and she was a straight freak. She was down for whatever in the sheets. "Yeah I remember you," he said smiling. "I apologize for not getting at you but I've been busy and outta town these last couple of months. But what the business is?" he asked. "Just trying to kick it and get away from this place. My bitch ass brother gone drive me crazy," she said sounding frustrated. He really didn't care about her personal problems but he asked anyway. "Oh ya, what's up in yo world?" "I'm just ready to get my own shit, this nigga think just cause he pay the bills for me and my mama to live good that he can run me." "Why you ain't got yo own pad? You 20 years old don't tell me you a mama's girl." She laughed, "Naw it ain't that. Lonzo be into so much in the streets and he over protective of me and my moms," she explained. Nephew heard the name Lonzo and he got on guard. His mind started racing, thinking her brother was not the same Lonzo he's been looking for. He had to investigate more. He was so caught up in his thought process that he didn't hear Tiffany calling his name. "Hello Nephew," she yelled in the phone. "Oh my bad, what were you saying?" he asked. "Me and his bitch got into a scuffle, I hate that bitch Lina, she thank she a boss bitch or something," Tiffany explained. Nephew smiled when his insinuation was confirmed. Tiffany was his key to Lonzo! All types of shit was going through his head at the moment so he had to wrap this conversation up. "Hellloooo," Tiffany said in an annoyed tone due to him zoning out. "Nephew," she yelled. "My bad shawty, I think them bars still have affect on me. But hey from now on call me D-Will, Nephew was some shit I made up," he said giving her his initials to keep her from blurting out his name around Lina or Lonzo. "Ok D-Will, baby I'll call you whatever long as I can taste that candy cane again," she said seductively. "Oh ya that's fa sho; I'm in H-Town right not but I'll be back tomorrow so I'm def gone get at you. Keep that mouth and pussy wet for me ma." "That's a bet D-Will, just make sure them handle bars don't get the best of you cause I need you to be fully in tune with what I am gone do to you daddy," she said moaning in the phone.

Once they hung up Nephew fell back into his deep thoughts. At first he entertained the thought that Lonzo may have found out he was involved with his sister and had her call and try to set him up but he dismissed it due to the hatred in her voice when she spoke of Lonzo. But he still knew he had to play it safe.

*　　*　　*

On the ride back to Dallas KB was thinking about the best move to eliminate Profit and the remainder of his crew. Guillotine kept him informed on Profit's wild out moves. The fool ran up in Diaz's spot with his goons and killed his connect along with two of his associates. That shocked KB since Diaz was such an important factor in Dallas. Guillotine informed him that Profit and Pedro were at war and Pedro was coming up with the short end of the stick, shedding the most blood. KB thought about letting them go at it in hopes that Pedro would knock him off but he dismissed that thought. From the information being brought to KB, it seems Profit was robbing and killing anybody that he felt was rolling in bread. That meant KB and his crew were targets. Even though they made a truce a while back didn't mean shit. KB still saw him as an enemy.

KB and his crew were able to enjoy a couple of months in Houston and bring back a half of million with them. KB couldn't do nothing but smile to himself for the accomplishments him and his boys made. He knew the battle wasn't over so he kept gaming his crew to stay alert and not get too comfortable.

*　　*　　*

CHAPTER 17

Nephew was spending some much needed time with the twins. They were hanging out and fucking with some bad bitches. Nephew didn't mind breaking bread with his little bros. It wasn't nothing like loyalty between the family and in times like these, it brought them closer together. Nephew was also making get aways with Tiffany as they engaged in some much needed booty calls. She turned out to be a cool individual but he knew he couldn't get attached because the time was approaching for him to make his move on Lonzo.

Nephew had just scooped up Tiffany from the house in North Dallas. It was 2:00 in the morning when Nephew and his bros just left the club. He didn't want to end his night so soon and since Kayla was out of town, he didn't want to spend the night alone. For that reason he opted to spend it with Tiffany. For some reason or another it seemed like Tiffany was in another world. They had spoken very little since he had picked her up. They were cool so Nephew was somewhat concerned. "What's up shawty?" Nephew asked rubbing her thigh. Tiffany was rocking a beige Baby Phat mini-skirt with the matching top, and some beige and white flat top Baby Phat shoes. She jumped when Nephew touched her, "huh, what you say baby?" 'Damn you alright tonight?" he asked. "Yeah just a lot on my mind, when you get to Forest Lane will you stop at that 7-11 for me?" Nephew nodded and blew her actions off. He pulled up in the 7-11 and parked on the side by a dumpster so he could roll a much needed blunt. Before Tiffany hopped out the car, he could have sworn he saw a tear roll down her cheek. *"Women, so emotional,"* he thought.

He was so caught up in rolling his blunt he didn't see the masked gunman creeping on his passenger side. His light came on and before everything registered, he was looking down the barrel of a humongous .50Cal Dessert Eagle. "Nigga if you don't want your brains sitting on that," the gunman said as he disarmed Nephew and relieved him of his gun. "You see that white Benzo right there? Follow it and if you do anything I wouldn't do, the .50 gone sound off," the gunman insinuated. Nephew cursed himself for getting caught slipping like this. He could hear his uncle's voice. *"Slippers count."* Nephew put the Escalade in reverse and pulled behind the white Benz. How and who was running through his head but all curiosity was confirmed when he saw Tiffany walk out the store and hop in the back seat of the Benz. He had been set up! Tiffany turned around and they locked eyes. Nephew could see the hurt in her eyes and all he could do was shake his head in disgust. He knew Lonzo was behind this if Tiffany was involved. Blood was thicker than water and it was truly showing. As he followed the Benz he contemplated a lot of things but when he looked to his right and saw that cannon pointed at his gut, he ceased all thoughts.

The gunman looked around before taking off his mask and smiling at Nephew. "Surprise nigga," he said. It was Lonzo's right hand man, Ra-Ra. "You look shook nigga," he said holding the gun steady on Nephew. Nephew occasionally looked Ra-Ra's way to assure him he didn't fear him. "Man I can't believe you was falling for a bitch like Tiffany but then again I could; the bitch can suck a dick can't she?" he said laughing. Nephew gazed at Ra-Ra, gritting his teeth. "Oh don't tell me you was falling for that well trained hoe'" he said. Nephew thought, how could Ra-Ra sit there and talk so reckless about his best friend's sister. "Do you talk this reckless bout Lonzo sister in front of him?" Nephew asked. "Sister," Ra-Ra said laughing. "You fell for that lame ass shit, Nigga you really are lame." That ain't Lonzo's sister as matter of fact her, Bre-Bre, LaNay, Lina and a couple of other hoes are under Lonzo's guidance; Nigga he the pimp, they were the hoes and you the trick that got played," he said laughing. Nephew was furious, broiling hot on the inside. He was messed up, he didn't see the signs. Ra-Ra saw him in a zone and decided to fuck with him some more. "Yeah nigga! Lina selling that pussy too, the mother of yo seed nigga, that's some shit ain't it?" Ra-Ra said, shaking his head in disgust. "Oh and we not fucked up bout BT or Crew, we sat that shit up so y'all can knock them rat ass niggas off; but when you somehow got them hoes to leave with you we started formulating our plan," he explained.

Nephew reached for his freshly rolled blunt, "Whoa whoa whoa, what you doing nigga?" Ra-Ra said putting the gun to Nephew's head. Nephew held up the blunt and Ra-Ra allowed him to fire it up. They pulled up to some apartments called Stoney Brook and drove to the back. Nephew was instructed to park the Escalade behind the Benz. Before he could cut the ignition off somebody opened the driver side and snatched him out the seat. They had a .20 gage pointed in his face. "Nigga walk!" he ordered. He heard another voice tell somebody to get rid of the Escalade. He walked past the Benz and tried to see through the tint but couldn't see shit. They led him to a downstairs two bedroom apartment. Once they got him in the apartment they strapped him to a chair, handcuffing both feet to the chair and bound his hands behind him. He was sitting in the middle of the living room. About 5 minutes later he heard the door open behind him and could hear whispering. He sat there with a mug on his face, letting his foes know that he wasn't the least bit scared. "Sit down on the couch and don't say shit," he heard Lonzo tell somebody. He smelled the mixture of women perfume, weed and liquor. Lonzo stepped in Nephew's face and smiled. "Well, well, well look what the trap caught. I can't believe this shit," he said smiling. Nephew just held his mug. "Oh you ain't so tough now huh nigga?" Lonzo barked. "Nigga fuck you. Do what you gone do and get this shit over with," Nephew said with much venom.

Ra-Ra stepped from the side and hit Nephew across the face with the butt of his gun, opening a dash under his eye. "You might want to shut the fuck up," Lonzo said. "Nephew felt his blood trickling down his face but he didn't bow down. "Suck my dick simp ass nigga," Nephew said. Ra-Ra struck him again with the pistol then followed with a barrage of haymakers. Nephew felt himself slipping into darkness. His face and body was numb. Blood leaked from four open gashes. His white and gray Gino shirt was now covered in blood. Lonzo turned his chair around and Nephew was now facing three females, Bre-Bre, LaNay, and Tiffany. "You hoes see this? If y'all don't get with the program y'all gone end up like this," he said, punching Nephew and knocking blood from his mouth. "If you go to the police I'll go to your family and serve them in the same manner, one by one," he said punching Nephew again.

With every punch blood flew. The girls turned their heads because they had never seen so much blood. Tears ran down Tiffany's cheeks because she really had feelings for Nephew. "Ok Lonzo," she said. "Is all this necessary to get a point across?" she asked wiping her face. "Bitch don't ever question me, stand yo ass up," he barked. As she stood up he slapped her sending her to the ground. "Bitch don't turn business personal, now you hoes get outta my face and go make some money." After hearing Lonzo ramble for about ten minutes, Nephew had strength to stay conscious. Somebody knocked on the door and when he saw who entered, everything made sense.

*   *   *

KB had been calling Nephew's phone since 2:00am. He was warning his people to stay on their toes after learning that Profit had teamed up with some more niggas and they were all targets. The streets were talking and he didn't want nobody making the front page of Dallas Morning News. It was KB's duty to make sure everybody was sharp. He had been calling

Nephew for the past couple of hours but grew restless. The twins said he was on a booty call with some chic named Tiffany so he decided he would chill until he heard anything further.

*　　*　　*

"Damn y'all done beat the nigga half to death," The unknown voice said. Nephew was slipping in and out of darkness. "Man just chill Profit, I owed him that ass whooping," Lonzo said. "Oh that's how you got that scar over your eye huh," Profit said laughing. He squatted in front of Nephew; "Damn man y'all took this shit too far," Profit said looking at Nephew's polarized face. Nephew had two swollen eyes, busted lips, and a broken nose. Blood dripped from his mouth and nose as he sat slumped in the chair. Profit shook Nephew trying to get him to focus on him. Nephew tried to focus but he was out of it. "Hey hey this what's going on; We holding you for a ransom so you pretty much know how this shit go so just go with the flow," Profit said standing up. "Did y'all make that call?" he asked Lonzo as he puffed on a Newport. "Naw we left that for you to do," Lonzo answered as he handed him Nephew's phone.

*　　*　　*

CHAPTER 18

BJ and Lisa just finished sharing a passionate moment and he loved every minute of it. She proved to be very loyal to BJ and he began to trust her more and more as time progressed. There was nothing he wanted more than a ride or die chic to hold his fort down. BJ received a call from KB a couple of hours ago telling him to stay razor sharp because shit was hot in the streets and their crew was the main target. BJ knew that the rules in the game were not fair and whatever goes up must come down. He knew he had done a lot since being released from T.D.C. but he didn't want his fate dealt to him by another man or foe, he knew Karma was a motha.

Lisa was in the shower while BJ was in the game room shooting a solo pool game. He was glad Lisa was around to help him keep his mind at ease while he kept a low profile. He hadn't heard from Kerri and his mind would often daydream about her sex game. She was very seductive and submissive. He loved the way she called his name during sex sessions. But oh well, he just took it as a lost. Bitches in the game come and go.

He was snapped out of his trance when he heard a loud crash and gunfire coming from his living room. His mind started ticking after it clicked that somebody was here to serve him his death warrant. He knew he had to make it to his pistols in the next room. He peeped around the corner and saw two masked men tearing up his spot. He got low and sprinted to a room across the hall. *"Bak . . . Bak . . . . Bak . . . . Bak . . . . Bak"* The gunman spit round after round as his target sprinted from one room to the other. BJ made it to his twin Glock 40's and went into military mode, *"Bak . . . Bak . . . Bak . . . Bak."* One of the gunmen was firing recklessly from behind the wall so BJ ducked behind his china cabinet where he could see his target in the doorway. His thoughts went to Lisa so he knew he had to make a move, not just any move, but a smart move and he knew he had to do it fast. One of the gunmen stepped around the corner and hit the room up with gun shots. BJ saw an open opportunity and took it, *"Bak . . . Bak . . . Bak . . . Bak . . . Bak . . . Bak."* The gunman dropped in the doorway with four slugs in his corpse. "Come on out mothafucka," he heard the other gunman yell along with Lisa screaming in the background. BJ stepped around the corner and saw the gunman had a chrome .38 Special pointed at Lisa's head. "Nigga drop yo pistol or I'm gone send this bitch to meet yo other bitch," he said. BJ twisted his face at the gunman as he held his position. "Yeah nigga that's right; it's very unfortunate yo girl had to be the one to die for yo actions. But you fucked up when you robbed me and my partner and let us live." "Man let her make it this is between us," BJ said. The gunman took his mask off and revealed his identity. "Yeah nigga, it's me, the almighty Memphis."

BJ kicked himself for letting him live. Now the shit came back to haunt him and it cost Tara her life. "Nigga you know the streets talk and them masks don't do a nigga no good. Ya boy Baby Jay let his riches get the best of him," Memphis said smiling. "You killed Baby Jay," BJ asked. "Unfortunately, but you can thank Profit for that price. For 80G's, I woulda killed my mama. Two birds with one stone," he said as he shook his head. "Now it's time for you to check out," aiming his pistol at BJ. Lisa didn't hesitate and went for the gun, "*Bak . . . Bak*"

Two shots went to the ceiling as Memphis and Lisa wrestled with each other. He over powered her to get the gun and shot her. BJ saw the opening and let off eight shots, dropping Memphis where he stood. Lisa was lying in a pool of blood as BJ ran to her side. Before he knew it police flooded his apartment, "Drop your weapon, drop your weapon," they yelled. He put his gun down and laid next to Lisa as a tear rolled down his cheek.

*   *   *

Profit had masterminded one of the best plans ever. All he had to do now was keep the ball rolling. By now half of KB crew should be looking at their eyelids. He had hits on a spot that was ran by Bam, Velt, and George. He also had another spot ran by LD, Marcus, and J-Note. Profit flipped open the Sprint phone and made his call.

*   *   *

KB rolled over and checked the clock. It was 8:00 in the morning. His cell phone was ringing off the hook. He reached over Stacy to grab his phone to see the called ID read, Nephew. "Nigga where the fuck you been?" KB barked. "Whoa partna slow ya roll," Profit said, smiling. "What! Who is this? Put Nephew on the phone and quit playing," KB ordered. "I would put him on the phone but he's all tied up," Profit said, laughing. "Man stop playing fucking games! Who is this? KB asked in a frustrated tone. The voice on the other end continued to laugh, "Look niiga let's get down to business. I know the streets been putting the word out so you know I've been on yo ass huh! I shouldn't have to say no more."

KB sat straight up in the bed as he put a face with the familiar voice. "Profit where's my Nephew?" "I told you he was tied up at the moment. Now if you ever wanna see him again you'll shut the fuck up and listen. By now the majority of your team should be part of the past so it's me and you homeboy," Profit said. "I want a quarter mill by tonight or kinfolk dead," he said boldly. "Where the fuck I'm gone get that kinda cash from?" KB asked, playing his part. "I don't know nigga pull it out ya ass but I do know this one thing; you better have that cash ready by 11:30 tonight cause come midnight baby gone be in the Trinity somewhere and don't try to get nobody else involved," he ordered. "Fuck you nigga I'm a G, I handle my own matters. Let me talk to my Nephew," KB demanded. He was so heated invisible smoke was coming from his head. Shit was ugly and he knew it was about to be a lot of blood shedding. Profit put the phone to Nephew's ear, "Speak nigga." KB heard raspy breathing in the phone and knew at that moment Nephew was not in good health. "Nephew!" KB barked in the phone.

"Don't . . . . pay . . . ." Nephew said through swollen lips. "What? What you say?" KB asked, struggling to hear Nephew. "Don't . . . . pay . . . ." Nephew said again as Profit snatched the phone away from his face. KB knew at that point that Nephew was on his last leg. "Get that money nigga, I'll call you back with a location," Profit barked before hanging up in KB's face.

*   *   *

CHAPTER 19

KB sat there in a daze, thinking about how shit came to this. He knew but he didn't want it to end like this. He had plans to be a self-made millionaire along with his crew. He vowed to get money by all means but never had he pictured things crumbling like this. He should have killed Profit a long time ago but gave him the benefit of doubt after the truce, now it was costing him.

"Baby what's wrong?" Stacy asked as she looked into KB's eyes. "Look, shit is getting crazy right now so I need you to get on the phone and book you a flight to mama's place. Don't ask questions just do it baby," he said getting out of bed. He tried calling BJ but didn't get an answer. Then he tried LD, no answer. Guillotine, no answer. "Fuck! This shit can't be happening," he yelled. *[Knock . . . . knock . . . . knock]* "Baby grab that pistol and get in the closet. If anybody come in there besides me, empty the clip," he explained as he picked up both of his Glock .45's. "Baby what's up?" Satcy asked. "Just do what I said," he yelled. She went into the spacious closet and KB made his way to the front with both of his guns ready to blaze. *[Bam . . . Bam . . .*

Bam] . . . . KB looked out the peep hole and relaxed when he saw who it was. He tucked one of his pistols and opened the door. Guillotine and Bam rushed in the house. "Why the fuck y'all ain't been answering y'all phones?" KB barked. Bam sat on the couch and buried his face in his palms. Guillotine paced the living room floor. "Man what's up?" KB asked. "Bro everybody dead! Velt, George, J-Note and Marcus. I've been trying to call LD but I can't find him nowhere," Guillotine said as he lit a Newport. "Me and Bam been fuckin with Low all night. We took him a half of brick and when we hit our spots, shit was chaotic. Police every damn where," Guillotine said.

KB went numb. He thought Profit was trying to shake him up when he said he hit his team up. But the shit was real. "Have y'all heard from BJ?" KB asked. "We went by his spot and rolled up just in time to see the paramedics rolling three bodies out his spot. Shit didn't look too good," Bam said. KB had to catch a seat when he got weak at the knees. He had to pull himself together so he could come up with a proper plan. From the looks of it, Guillotine and Bam were all he had left.

*   *   *

BJ had been sitting in the interrogation room for the last two hours chain smoking cigarettes. He hadn't heard any info on his status, all he knew was that they were charging him with double homicide. But that wasn't what was bleeding in his mind; all he could think about was Lisa. She sacrificed her life for his life. If it wasn't for her brave move he would be laid out on a steel bed. He put his head on the table and shed a tear for Lisa. He also thought about Lizzarha growing up without a mother in a cold world. He wished that his story could have ended happily ever after but when you live the life he lived there were only two outcomes; death or jail. He escaped death many of times and in his heart he knew it was the prayers of his mother that spared his life. BJ was raised in the church and he knew this life was not the life but the streets will draw you in if you let them. He didn't regret anything he had done up until now but the thought of going back to jail was taunting him. He vowed to beat poverty and live how he wanted to live by all means. He would let nothing or nobody stop him but reality was setting in. His thoughts were interrupted when two detectives walked in. One stood at the door and the other sat at the table across from him. They held each other's gaze before the detective broke the silence. "I'm Detective Garcia and behind you is my partner Detective Morrison. As you can see we work homicide," Garcia explained. "Now we put your story into prospective and how things went down but for the time being we have to follow proper procedures. "Procedures?" BJ said, twisting his face up. "It's clear that two mothafuckas kicked my door down, killed my girl, and tried to kill me. Fuck procedures! The truth and what's real is in plain view," BJ said, angry that after all he just went through these two pigs were screaming procedures. "Whoa, whoa, just calm down," Detective Garcia said. "Let me finish. We just got a word that your girlfriend Lisa was going to be alright," he said. When BJ heard Lisa and alright in the same sentence he couldn't believe it. "I thought she was dead," BJ said. "When paramedics arrived on the scene she was merely unconscious. She received a shot to the lower back that went in and came out of her side. She lost a lot of blood but managed to pull through. She is being investigated at this time and if her story matches yours we'll present the information to Grand Jury along with the outcome of the crime scene investigation and you could walk away in self defense," Garcia explained.

BJ felt like new life was breathed into him. A tear of joy rolled down his cheek as he started to think about Lisa. "Detective can I get a phone call?" he asked. He had to call KB and let him know what was going on.

*   *   *

LD was lurking outside of one of Profit's spots. He was strapped with two Tech .95, with thirty rounds in each clip. The previous night he managed to escape Profits failed attempt to take his life but Marcus and J-Note were less fortunate. LD was able to get info out of one of the gunmen before pumping him full of lead. The information was a compass to his target, and now he was waiting for him to come out.

LD thought about how he got to this point in his life. All his life he was a loner and nobody cared enough to embrace him when he was a young troubled boy. At the age of 15 he witnessed countless of murders, at 17 he committed his first murder and the numbers continued to rise. He grew up around death so he embraced it as if it was a part of his family. LD appreciated his friendship with Nephew because he was the only one that ever showed him that he cared. For that reason, LD swore to ride or die for him. He was introduced to Nephews "all means" tactics and made a vow with Nephew to get rich or die trying.

He felt death knocking at his door and was not hesitant to open the door and face the challenge. That is the reason he was sitting outside his enemy's house in broad day light at 3:00 in the evening. The door opened and his target emerged with his protégé and cousin. LD got out his car and walked across the street.

Bren, Creep, and Barry had just stepped out the house heading to North Dallas to meet up with Profit so that they could close a chapter to their book of enemies. By this time tomorrow they figured they would be laid up in ATL somewhere. *[Bak . . . Bak . . . Bak . . . Bak . . . Bak . . . Bak . . . Bak . . .]*, all laughter ceased when the sounds of gunshots brought the trio back to reality; they were caught off guard. Barry was a quick draw and was able to get behind the S.U.V. and draw down. Creep wasn't so lucky; he got hit up six times before his body hit the ground. *[Bak . . . Bak . . . Bak . . . Bak . . . Bak . . . Bak . . . Bak . . .]*, LD fired round after round. Bren tried to make it back in to the house but was hit at the door. *[Bak . . . Bak . . . Bak . . . Bak,* blood splattered on the wall as his lifeless body crumpled to the floor. *[Click, click, click]*, LD dropped one of his Techs and loaded the other. Just as he got the clip in and cocked it, he was met with a barrage of slugs that sent him to the ground. LD laid in his own blood prepared to walk through eternal darkness. He locked eyes with his enemy and smiled. *[Bak]*, Barry put a slug right between the monster's eyes. It was something about the way LD smiled that freaked him out. He knew he would remember that last encounter that would haunt him for the rest of whatever life he had left. He hopped in the S.U.V. and fled the scene.

* * *

CHAPTER 20

KB was able to gather up the quarter mill with the help of Bam and Guillotine. Bam and Guillotine coughed up half together without much of a cost. KB went in his stash and got the other 100G and waited patiently for the phone call. He couldn't believe that in less than an hour his whole team had fallen. He felt even worse that BJ got blasted. In the middle of his thought process his phone started ringing. The caller ID said Dallas County. He thought *"who could this be calling me from the county?"* Maybe it was LD. "Hello." "You have a collect call from BJ," the animated voice said. "If you want to accept the call press 1, if not then hang up," the recording said. KB sighed in relief to hear BJ's voice on the other end. "Damn dawg what's poppin?" KB asked. "Man bro I'm glad you answered. I couldn't reach nobody," BJ said. "What's really up? Damn nigga I thought you were dead bro. Bam and Guillotine said they rolled by your spot this morning and saw them folks rolling three bodies out that bitch," KB explained. BJ filled him in on all the action and what was going on at the present time. KB was impressed that BJ held it down like that. "You know ya boy gone survive by all means," BJ said laughing. "Aye but I just made it up stairs and my bond is $10,000. They hit me with felon in possession of a firearm. Come get me dawg." "Hey bro, I'm gone send Leila up there right now, I gotta handle some business." KB hated he had to leave BJ in the dark about what was going on but he didn't want to be careless and talk over the phones. "Call me when you get out and come straight to my spot," KB said. "I'm gone leave some info with Leila." "Bet. I'm gone have Leila take me to get my car then head up to Charlton to check on Lisa," BJ told him. "Alright bro be safe."

After they hung up KB informed Bam and Guillotine that BJ was in fact alive and in the county. He explained everything BJ told him. "I guess I taught him good with the haters," Bam said smiling. KB called Leila and told her to stop whatever she was doing and go to David's Bell Bond. She hit him with some more disturbing news about LD. She explained that the streets were labeling him a hood legend. LD managed to take out Bren and Creep in broad day light before getting took down. That, along with his reputation would have people talking for years.

It was pushing 9:45 PM and KB's phone finally rung with the destination info. He decided to play it safe and just pay the money. He had enough credit in the streets to where he could hunt Profit down at a later time. "Hello," KB answered. "Ya boy LD pulled a brave mothafuckin move today. He really hit me where it hurt but being that I know that wasn't yo call I'm not gone hold you accountable. Bring the money to the DFW Airport and when you get there I will let you know what to do next."

With that being said Profit hung up. KB thought about the location. Profit was smart enough to pick a spot where he could guarantee his safety and the airport was the perfect spot; a lot of people and a lot of police. KB, Guillotine, and Bam headed to DFW Airport. KB formulated a nice little plan to assure that the drop went as planned. He silently prayed to Allah that nothing extreme happened to Nephew. The money wasn't a big deal, that can be replaced but you only had one life to live. KB just hoped that the money would spare his Nephew.

About thirty minutes later KB swung the Lexus in the parking lot and as expected, things were busy. People, cars, police, and more people flooded the place. He rode around and found a parking spot and right as he parked his phone rung. "What's up?" he answered. "Take the suit case into the first entrance, when you get in take a left and you'll see escalators and stairs. Go up the stairs and to your right there is a restroom with three stalls. Put the money in the last stall and make your exit. When you come out take a left and head toward Anchor 8. You'll see your Nephew's Escalade. He's in the back tied up, the keys unda the driver's side tire. If I see anybody other than you following these instructions, shit gone get real ugly in DFW," Profit said. "Oh and leave your two goons in the car," he said before the line went dead.

KB explained to his boys what the deal was then he made a call. "Hey follow me when you see me and watch the bag. Just be cool and act normal like you just got off the plane," he explained. "Alright," replied the anonymous voice. KB followed the directions. He analyzed the faces but nobody looked out of the ordinary. He headed up the stairs with the D&G duffle bag full of cash. To his right he saw the restroom and did as he was told. When he exited he saw a fine Dominion beauty chatting on her phone. He smiled showing his $10,000 grill and kept it moving. She waved and kept talking on her phone.

*   *   *

Wild Cherry:

She was in place like she was told. When it came to KB she didn't ask why, she just ask where, when, and sometimes how depending on the situation. She saw him walk in the bathroom with the brown and white D&G bag and watched his fine ass walk out. They locked eyes and he flashed her his million dollar smile. Damn she loved that nigga. She had to remind herself that she was on a business trip.

About ten minutes passed before a 6'0 feet, brown skin cat walked out the bathroom with the D&G bag. She let him get a couple strides in front of her before tailing him. She grabbed her decoy luggage and followed him still talking on the phone.

*   *   *

Barry

He waited in the first stall undetected for the drop to be made. He saw KB put the D&G bag in the third stall and walked out as planned. Barry grabbed the bag and waited ten minutes before walking out, passing a fine Dominican beauty. He checked the crowd for any stalkers to make sure no one was following him. He smiled on the inside as he thought about getting his cut. He would finally be able to branch off from Profit and start his own empire. He thought about his boys from Dewberry and the thought of him running things soothed him.

*   *   *

Profit:

Profit watched from his spot as he saw his cousin Barry walk to his car. Profit smiled at the thought of the quarter mill. That was enough for him to relocate and hop back in the game. He had a lot of family in Austin, TX and he was very familiar with the area so it wouldn't take much for him to sew it up. As soon as Barry made it to the car he picked up his cash. He wasn't worried about no one seeing because he had his foes on the other side of the airport being watched. Everybody was accounted for. KB should be walking up on the Escalade and his two goons were still sitting in that pretty ass money green Lexus.

Profit made his was over to Barry's whip just as he was climbing in. Barry looked up confused, "What's up kinfolk? I thought you was gone chill in the cut?" he asked. "I was bro but it's been a change of plans," Profit said, pulling out a chrome .38 Special and put it to his temple. "Sorry cuz but this ain't enough to split four ways. Money is the root of evil." With that being said he put one in his dome knocking brain fragments across the dash.

*   *   *

Malique:

He watched from ten yards away as Profit made it over to Barry's car. With Wild Cherry's help he was able to get into position. Once Profit vanished to the passenger side of Barry's car, Malique stayed low and made his way to Profit's car. He let himself in and ducked in the back seat. He talked his Uncle KB into letting him put in some work and wasn't no better time than now. The situation had something to do with his brother so he felt he deserved to be part of the plan. The only problem was his part of the plan involved killing somebody. His stomach was doing flips because he never had to do any killing before. Bam had him strapped with a 9mm Beretta with a Wilson silencer on it. It was too late to back down now; it was his time to man up. He laid very low, crouched behind the seat as he waited for his target. Profit quickly made his way back to his car. He cautiously looked around at the pedestrians and saw that no one was watching him. He jumped in and put the key in the ignition. New visions popped into his mind. He fumbled with the keys trying to start the car when all of a sudden Malique put the steal to the back of his head. "What tha . . . ." Profit said startled, looking into the eyes of his maker through the rearview mirror. After all the planning he had done, he got played in the end and now he knew it was check out time. Coming up he was taught to get it "By All Means." It was either run game or get gamed, play or get played, hustle or get hustled; In this case he got played, beaten at his own game. For that split second he envied his foe for the ability to outsmart him . . . .

[sssp.sssp.sssp.sssp.sssp.sssp.] (sound of the silencer)
After the first squeeze splattered Profits head all over the dash, Malique got trigger happy and kept squeezing. After he scratched his itch he grabbed the bag and made his exit. He made it back to his car, hopped in and picked up Wild Cherry before making their getaway.

* * *

KB:

He made it back to Nephew's Escalade and found the key and hopped in. By now his master plan should be in motion, if not already accomplished. He climbed to the back and saw his Nephew in a bloody leaking mess. A tear streamed down his cheek as he observed the mess they'd made of Nephew. He untied him and propped him up in the back seat. "Nephew, Nephew," he said shaking him. Nephew tried to open his eyes but could only open them enough to see it was his uncle. He tried to smile but his lips cracked as he coughed. "Damn Nephew man, fuck!," KB yelled. We gotta get you some medical attention just hold on," KB said. Nephew spoke in a weak voice as he held the gash under his rib cage from where he was stabbed by Profit to make him slowly bleed to death. "Bro . . . . is . . . . this . . . . how it's . . . . suppose . . . . to . . . . end?" Nephew said as he wheezed for air. "Naw nigga. It don't stop right here, just fight this shit," KB said. "We . . . . had . . . . a . . . . pretty . . . . good . . . . run huh?" he asked, smiling through cracked lips. "Look nigga fuck that just stay focused," KB said, climbing in the front seat to crank the Escalade. He watched Nephew through the rearview mirror thinking, *"Not like this! We were good, ready to settle and get out the game and climb to higher heights. I guess it is true, live by the sword, die by the sword."* KB snapped out of his trance and called Guillotine to tell him to meet him at the Arlington Medical Center. Guillotine let him know that everything went as planned.

KB sped through the parking lot and down I-20. "Nigga shit gone be right Nephew. We gone open up them spots and do it big," KB said, trying to keep him conscious. "Make . . . . sure . . . . Twins . . . . make it," Nephew said. "Naw nigga you gone make sure. You gone be aight kid," KB said looking through the rearview mirror. Nephew smiled the best he could then took a deep breath. "Nigga you a G and we gone continue to climb the charts," KB said as he weaved through traffic. "By . . . . All . . . . Means," those were Nephew's last words as he rested his eye lids and welcomed the after world.

KB hadn't noticed that Nephew crossed over. He swung up in the lot of the medical center where Guillotine, Bam, Malique, and Wild Cherry stood front and center. He pulled up to the emergency exit and jumped out. "Somebody get a Doctor!" KB yelled. He opened the door to the Escalade and saw that Nephew was at peace. It hit him like a ton of bricks. Nothing would ever amount to his Nephew's life; not money, not revenge, not nothing. It was funny how things went down in the streets but when you in the grind for riches, death not a part of your plans. The biggest trick of the enemy is making one think that they're invincible to what is evitable. When you decide to live the life of the streets and in the streets, Death is reality. Unfortunately for KB, death played its roll and just like anyone else of the matter he had no other choice but to accept it.

Epilogue 8: Loose Ends

It had been six-months since the blood war between KB and profit took place. The streets were hot and the murder rate was up. Since then things had calmed down. KB was still dealing with Pedro and he still had his boys, chuck and James, doing their thing in Houston. Since nephew's death he'd opened up two after hour spots, one in Oak cliff which was operated by Bam and the other one in South Dallas, ran by Guillotine. He had a studio built in the back of the one in Oakcliff so the twins could do their rap thing. BJ was in the county serving 180 days for the guns he used to kill DJ and Memphis. He beat the murder cases with self defense. His girl Lisa was pregnant and stayed by his side, ride or die!

*   *   *

KB was ducked off in a dark corner in one of Tessca's V.I.P rooms. He watched as Wildcherry and Bay did their thing. Those two were the best bait a nigga could have on his team. They would use every tactic they knew to get a nigga to trust them.

It took KB six-months to catch up with the famous big pimpin Lonzo. He used Tiffany to get all the info he needed on him since KB didn't know much about him. Tiffany proved to be very valuable because her info was accurate. "Damn ya'll some bad Bitches!" Lonzo said as he felt Wildcherry up while she gave a butt naked lap dance. Baby was on the table dancing and rubbing herself. It took everything they had to lure Lonzo into their trap but it worked.

KB slipped his gloves on as he prepared to tie up the loose ends. He stepped out of the darkness but only Wildcherry and Bay could see him. He walked up behind Lonzo and that was Wildcherry's que to get up. "Hold up! Why you stop?" Lonzo asked, looking at Wildcherry as she smiled. KB grabbed him from behind in a vice grip choke-hold. He flexed his bicep muscles, cutting off Lonzo's air circulation. Lonzo tried to struggle with KB but it was no use. "This is a call from Nephew," KB whispered in Lonzo's ear. Lonzo gave up the fight and drifted into darkness. When Lonzo's body went limp, KB snapped his neck; a move, courtesy of Bam and his military tactics. They drug his body out the back exit unseen and tossed him in the trunk of the awaiting car. Everybody rode to the next destination, all he could think about was taking himself and his crew to New Heights . . . . *Stay Tuned . . . .*